Henrik Ibsen

Nora

A Doll's House - Et dukkehjem - a play. Translated from the Norwegian by Henrietta

Frances Lord

Henrik Ibsen

Nora
A Doll's House - Et dukkehjem - a play. Translated from the Norwegian by Henrietta Frances Lord

ISBN/EAN: 9783337188849

Printed in Europe, USA, Canada, Australia, Japan

Cover: Foto ©Andreas Hilbeck / pixelio.de

More available books at **www.hansebooks.com**

NORA;

OR, A DOLL'S HOUSE.

(ET DUKKEHJEM.)

A PLAY

BY

HENRIK IBSEN.

TRANSLATED FROM THE NORWEGIAN

BY

HENRIETTA FRANCES LORD.

New Edition, Revised.

GRIFFITH, FARRAN, OKEDEN AND WELSH,

NEWBERY HOUSE, CHARING CROSS ROAD, LONDON.

Lily Publishing House, Chicago, U.S.A.

1890.

PREFACE TO SECOND EDITION.

A Doll's House has been a decade before the public; yet criticism continues to rage around it. This might be accounted for, by saying the subject of Marriage is of universal interest, and any striking exposition of it will serve as a lesson book. But this is not the only reason *Nora* engages attention. The topic has come up for final settlement, in the sense, that the human race will never relapse into any one of its many shades of discomfort and falseness. And of this final settlement, *Nora*, and any similar expressions of sentiment, are signs, not causes.

Those who are grateful to Ibsen for writing the play, have thanked me only too kindly for translating it, ever since 1882, and for the introduction, in which I arranged the thoughts of 'Robinson,' a distinguished Swedish critic, because I thought his saying for us, just as Ibsen does, the same things that we women say for ourselves, was noteworthy. Many other noble men know that happiness for men in married life depends upon the freedom of women.

Criticism comes from (1) People who really dislike progress, change, improvement; (2) people who are timid about it and are sticklers for degree and method. The obstructionists I leave to learn on life itself. "The ship which will not learn by the rudder must learn on the rocks." *Nora* affects such persons uncomfortably, because it makes them feel searched and known. Verily, "*Thou hast searched me, and known me;*" by every passing event, every trifle,—even by a drama, perhaps read carelessly, which nevertheless will haunt the memory. It seems a forestalling of the Day of Judgment, when people expect to feel very uncomfortable; and they prefer to put off the evil day as long as possible. But since no day passes without our judging something, it is always 'the Day of Judgment'; and whenever our accounts have to be settled, we shall be asked whether we shirked warnings, hints, the realities of life brought before us.

I watched Miss Janet Achurch's magnificent performance of *Nora* in *A Doll's House*, in London, July 1889. It was announced to be 'translated by William Archer.' He has acknowledged in print his debt to me as the original translator of *Nora* and *Ghosts*. Appleton has republished *Nora* in America, no copyright law protecting me. I am content to leave all transgressors to that inexpe▓▓ moment just referred to,—the Day of Judgment.

Mr. Besant's imaginary termination of the ▓▓ dishonours every one concerned, as untruthful ▓▓ are sure to do. According to him, Helmer would drink and Nora would write bad novels. Mr. Besant should not think so badly of Helmer; and I hope he will be told this by men whom he respects. I leave them to settle their own account with him. Helmer would never sink thus; it is a most unnecessary assumption of Mr. Besant's. And if his idea of Helmer, the man, is so mistaken, it does not take much ability to see that in assuming Nora would write bad novels, he shows even less intuition. At the worst, Helmer would dessicate; becoming a mere dried mummy, a prig. If he did improve, he would become a fine man. But my heart sinks as I write the words; he was one of those who must wade through a shallow ocean of second-rateness on their way to what is clear and true. And would he tolerate Nora at his side meanwhile?

When I published my translation in 1882, the last

thing which occurred to me was, that ~~people would assume Nora never returned to her home.~~ Progressive but timid minds often assume this. How can they be so wanting in knowledge of human nature? *The Pall Mall Gazette*, ever brave in woman's cause, said in its literary jottings lately, that *A Doll's House* was a story from real life—that Nora returned when she had learnt her lesson, and has been at home nearly twenty years. I have always felt the play was based on real life.

Another assumption is, that Nora thought herself very wise. But Nora says plainly and humbly, "~~I~~ ~~t try to become a human being, and, in my~~ ~~ness and ignorance, a little solitude is what I~~

~~~~ ~~~~ontend that Ibsen regards her as a model ~~~~ wishes all wives to leave all husbands, ~~~~ satisfaction arises. That Ibsen knew one ~~~~ woman might act like Nora and another quite ~~~~ently, no one could doubt, who regarded him as ~~~~ student of realities. But, fortunately, we have a proof of this in the *Lady of the Sea* (1888). There the husband is kind and indulgent; the wife only needs to be told 'you are free,' and her nature turns to him with passionate eagerness. Just so would Nora have clung to Helmer, had he been the kind of man, who kneeling down by her, would have said gently, "Love, when anything goes wrong between us, some of it must be my fault; tell me what you think it is." There are plenty of men who are at least as good and sensible as this; and the Noras of the world recognize them as real helpmates, not owners or tyrants. Imagine Helmer a human, kind, intelligent man. But then such a man would never have let Nora build up a Doll's House for their joint home. Ibsen's point is: "Given a man of Helmer's ~~character~~ ~~and a woman of Nora's, their home~~ must be remodelled

before it can be built on a firm foundation." If this
be all Ibsen claims to indicate, it is beside the mark
to say, that another married couple would act differently; of course they would. It is equally beside the
mark to say, "Nora and Helmer are not like anybody
I know." This is very likely. Nora is a Norwegian
girl of middle-class life. She is not the wealthy young
woman of the best English or American society, who
has visited in large country houses, had a maid to
dress her hair, had quantities of offers, and hosts of
friends. Nor is Nora the serious benevolent girl, who
till marriage, employs her time usefully in a large circle
of relatives and friends. Nor is she the woman who
is very admirable, but 'not quite a lady,' like
Christina Linden; who knows the world just as it is.
All these types get social education; Nora had none.
Nora is not what sensible mothers and aunts call a
well brought-up young lady. How should she be?
Ibsen does not bring forward a single relative on
Helmer's side, and alludes to Nora's deceased father
as the only kin she had. Nora was not rich enough
to visit in society much, after her marriage; and
Helmer discouraged her from even talking of the few
ties her school days had yielded her. Serious people
do not admire Nora; because her fibs—as about
eating contraband maccaroons and the greediness
implied—blind them to her sterling worth in resisting
help from Dr. Rank after his declaration of love; her
power of keeping her painful secret about the loan
from Krogstad; her untiring industry in her home.
Frivolous people do not admire Nora because of this
sterling worth; it reproaches them. A serious sensible woman, would never have left husband and
children; but neither would she have forged a name
from good motives. No critics are so mistaken as
those who think Nora went because she was selfish.
A selfish woman never leaves her bread and butter;

her respectable husband; her position, (just improved by his appointment as bank manager). Nora was absolutely unselfish, noble-hearted, and misinformed. Helmer was misinformed without being unselfish or noble-hearted. Nora went away from fear of again harming those she loved by her ignorance; this danger over, she would fly home. She would find some work; in three months she would long to be tossing Emmy in her arms; in six months she would be homesick; but she would resolve to hold out for one year; her idea of self-respect, purpose, industry would prompt that; by the time autumn came, she would be making notches on a stick to count the days, and she would come home of her own accord to spend Christmas.

The greatest difficulty would be with Helmer. Such a man really likes a conventional woman for his wife; a woman who does and says just what others do and say. He is perfectly sincere in his preference for what is second-rate; and I am always sorry for him, when he is married to a woman, who wants to be more real, and to find realities instead of seemings. Life would never run easily between Nora and Helmer, because they do not desire the same things. Helmer quite frankly wishes for Conventionality; Nora with equal frankness would wish for 'real things'; only to have friends she really valued, and only to spend money on objects she and her husband really admired; not to spend for the sake of possessing just what other people consider desirable. Nora would wish her children to study according to preference, Helmer according to custom. If Emmy disliked music, Nora would let her learn drawing instead; Helmer would fear Emmy's 'peculiar tastes.' Nora perhaps dislikes the army as a profession; but would promote Ivar's adopting it, because she respects his tendencies and wishes him to choose his own path. She could not consent except on this principle, or in silence.

Helmer would be annoyed at her way of arriving at
her duty in the matter; and would long for a wife
who would take the same view of the army as other
people do, or who would at least say she did. Bob
would wish to go into business. Some divergence
would occur over that event. Helmer would incline
to paying the premium instead of finishing Emmy's
education. Nora, remembering her own half-taught
girlhood, might plead for some other way of doing the
thing. And having tried self-effacement for eight years,
she would never dare to solve her difficulties by acting only 'so as to please Torvald'; and she is too
generous and 'real' to suggest his effacing himself a
little to please her. She would desire he should act
only as he thinks right; and yet he would never go to
the bottom of things with her; or he might even try
to do so; but what he would fish up and present her
as a pearl of truth, would merely be a "By the bye,
you know, Jones was quite right the other day. He
said, 'I find I come out all right when I do exactly
what Smith does.' Depend upon it, my dear Nora,
there is sound sense in what Jones says." Helmer
would really succeed best in life by acting much as
others do; he would feel truest to himself thus;
happiest; and prepared to learn from mistakes; because they would be made along a path his conscience
approves : Conventionality. He would then announce
things as 'discoveries,' which Nora's intuitions and
love of principle had taught her years before; but he
would never see she had learned them by these
methods; nor that this was the cause of her quiet
manner on his announcing his 'discoveries.'

In 1882, when I issued the first large edition of
Nora, I had no counter-solution to propose for Dr.
Rank's view on Heredity; but without saying a word
in challenge of it, I cannot issue the present one.
Now, however, the doctrine, "we reap as we sow,"

and not only in one existence but in many, seems to me truer than Heredity. Every soul on coming to this world, brings with it its own possibilities of harvest. 'Attraction of similar tendencies' accounts for peculiarities when exhibited in a whole family. A useful name for 'harvest' in this sense of evolution, is Karma, the Indian philosophical name for it; and as Ibsen's drama *Ghosts* turns on Heredity, my preface to it will be the proper place to treat the doctrines of Heredity and Karma.

. A good deal of present day discussion on marriage would gain in clearness and usefulness, if people knew whence arises their increased disposition to discuss it at all. That true marriage is a union of souls, hearts, minds, has been often stated. This is an echo of a deeper truth which has also been stated, but never quite satisfactorily. The truest marriage can only take place when the souls really belong to each other, were created to complete each other, are Twin Souls, or soul mates.

It is only the dullest minds who would not admit our Age to be one of transition from some older order to a new one. As a part of this transition, the fountains of the great deep having been broken up, certain restrictions upon human knowledge have come to a natural end; many a soul in the Unseen World is free to seek its mate still on earth; many such recognitions are attempted; many succeed, (the degree of conscious recognition varies;) with the result, that these divinely united souls radiate ideas of what true marriage should be, and these ideas are caught up by thousands and echoed in their hearts. And equally of course 'the Enemy' uses evil-disposed persons to desecrate this holy truth, and promote license within wedlock or outside it, alleging the attraction of 'soul-union' for what is only common-place improper conduct—which is the last thing 'soul-union' could possibly prompt.

The union of the Twin souls in earthly marriage is not a very common occurrence; and is not easy to distinguish from any other happy marriage characterized by good feeling, loyalty, and courage.   But where the two really belong to each other, the world often recognizes the fact with a very unexpected gleam of perception.

Regarding *A Doll's House* as a story of real life, I would describe Mrs. Linden and Krogstad as twin souls.   Their life-struggle side by side would be full of sweetness to them, and would purify both, until in old age they would know theirs was an eternal marriage.   Whether on earth or in the Unseen, your twin may not be 'perfect' or 'so good as you are'; and if on earth, it may be, that under the discipline of patience with your imperfect earthly partner, you are actually ministering to the one soul destined to share the rest of your evolution in endless future time.   Nora and Helmer were not Twin souls.   But, like all who have chosen each other in marriage, they owed each other the best either had to give.   Helmer gave his best in working for Nora's bread.   Nora thought she had given her best in borrowing money to save his life; and when she found that was wrong, it was still under the idea of doing the very best by her husband and her children, that she left them for a little while; though, as she said truly, the duty to our own soul, taught us by the conscience within each of us, must always have the first claim as guide of action.

> "*to thine own self be true,*
> *And it shall follow, as the Night the Day,*
> *Thou canst not then be false to any man.*"

FRANCES LORD.

Kensington, London,
March 1890.

LIFE OF HENRIK IBSEN.

HENRIK IBSEN was born in Norway, March 20, 1828, and
lived there until 1864, when, in his distress that Sweden and
Norway would not help Denmark to resist Prussia, he wrote
scornful epigrams about his fellow-countrymen; and since then
he has not been in Norway. He lived for some years in Dresden,
since 1878 has been chiefly in Rome, but has no settled home.

Of his earlier works, *Catilina*, *Fru Inger*, *The Comedy of Love*,
and above all, *Rivals for the Crown*, 1864, were those that chiefly
brought him into notice, until in 1866, *Brand* gave him a fame
that grew with *Peer Gynt*, *Youth's Band*, *Emperor and Galilean*
(translated by Miss C. Ray : S. Tinsley), *The Pillars of Society*;
1879 *Nora* appeared, and at Christmas 1881, *Ghosts*.

He has married a daughter of Mrs. Magdalene Thoresen, a
Norwegian poetess. He has a small literary pension from the
Norwegian Government, the rest of his income is derived from
▓▓▓▓▓ings.

▓▓▓▓ong gray hair and whiskers make him look somewhat more
▓▓▓. He is short, but firmly and well built, so that he looks
▓▓n he is. The most characteristic points in his serious
▓▓▓face, are his powerful forehead, which is remarkably
▓▓▓d high, a very Jupiter's brow, and his delicate mouth;
▓▓▓▓lips, but shuts energetically in a fine line, and it expresses
▓▓▓▓ble will, as though some giant resolve were for ever
▓▓▓▓n afresh. His small blue eyes almost disappear behind
▓▓▓▓les. His nose is quite Northern in its irregularity. He
▓▓▓▓ softly, moves slowly, and rarely gesticulates. His self-
command almost amounts to coldness; it is but the snow that
covers a volcano of wild and passionate power.

The play now given us as *Nora* is called in Norwegian *Et
Dukkehjem*. To a public unused to Ibsen's surprises, *A Doll's
House* is a misleading title; the German translator seems to have
felt this too, and preferred to call his translation of the play *Nora*.
Whatever is written in Swedish, Norwegian, or Danish can be
read without a translator's help in Norway, Sweden, Denmark,
and Finland; and, as I learnt during my own residence in Stock-

holm, 1878-9, the cultivated homes among these ten millions of people look to Ibsen as their great teacher. They do not always like what he says, but they let him speak on. Such furious discussion did *Nora* rouse when the play came out, 1879-80, that many a social invitation given in Stockholm during that winter bore the words, " You are requested not to mention Ibsen's *Doll's House!* " The play's firm hold on the Scandinavian mind has been strengthened, rather than effaced, by his *Ghosts* (1881); and how firm this hold is, a mass of criticism shows, as it continues to pour from the press. In a series of essays called ' Questions of the Day,' is *Ibsen and the Marriage Question*, by ' Robinson.' It explains Ibsen's position in the worlds of thought and literature, and in Scandinavian estimation so well, that I venture to give much of its substance.

Marriage is still an unsettled problem. The Eastern poets sing Woman a slave, the Western, Man enslaved by her. But far-sighted spirits like Dante, reject both views, and sing Ideal Love, a thought too precious for humanity to let it escape, when once it reached human consciousness. Yet it is philosophers and moralists whom Time leads to accept it, while the poets, its first leaders, ignore the truth that marriage involves human dignity, responsibility, community, and mutual trust. It is to making this truth clear that Henry Ibsen has devoted his poet's gift. No sooner does a great and popular poet do so, than we see how little woman's own voice has been heard in other poetry ; and we feel thankful that a singer who can make himself gladly heard, is singing of freedom, openness, true and conscious devotion, conscience responsible to itself alike in man and woman. Ibsen sees the world deluged by masculine qualities ; he approves them if, by devotion to a distinct plan and its execution, they touch heroism, otherwise he chases lovers of self mercilessly about with scorn or laughter. He sees womanly qualities hidden, fled away, or misunderstood. He does not construct some purely harmonious circumstances, and show Woman attaining a seeming equilibrium, and becoming all that her nature is capable of. He either shows her driven to crime or eccentricity by cramped or misdirected development (as Nora was), or losing her womanliness by being reared in a wrong state of society (like Helen in *Emperor and Galilean*) ; or finally he opens all the great gates of his poetry to noble, pure-hearted, loving, disappointed women, who move about among reckless men as the natural centres for conversion and reconciliation, but either lack courage to seize the occasion, or, if they have much courage, happen to have such a pig-headed, one-sided manhood to deal with, that the inspired woman, the heavenly herald of nature and conscience, is trampled under foot, or passed by, the man regretting it, but when it is too late.

Such are most of Ibsen's women. He considers they are to be found everywhere, a latent force whose accession humanity needs, and that his task is to release the Sleeping Beauty, as the prince did in our childish fable. The thorny wood has grown all round. Meanwhile, unwomanliness flaunts outside; the thorns are blooming. Men dream away life amid this injury to womanhood; at any rate they forget to break their way in to reality; they are ready for any deed rather than that. Ibsen approaches the thorn-girt home; he knows that every expression crushes thousands of conventionality's roses; and on his plain but trusty sword are these words only: Love and Understand. Expanded, the words mean—The union between two people is only true according as they love and understand each other, in thought, feeling, and will, tasks of duty and sources of joy; and are consequently able to fight life's battles, bear its pains, and enjoy its glory together; and this by having directed, forwarded, and freed each other's development.

Renowned as Ibsen has long been, it was *Nora* (1879, during a few months' journey round Europe) that procured him the title 'Woman's Poet,' because it threw a light on the path over all his past writing.

To see Ibsen's position as a dramatist, we ought to glance at the history of the stage, and especially at the French stage, which has influenced all other dramatic writing for the past 150 years, and then we shall ask why Ibsen passes by and turns away from something by which Frenchmen produce their greatest stage effects. That class of women to whom novels and plays have been giving complete publicity year after year, and who are very conspicuous in the world, are almost excluded from the great Northman's works. While French dramatists and their disciples are never weary of depicting these beings,—who have nothing of woman but her outward enchantment, whereby they rule Society's life, and are like a pest in its midst,—Ibsen has worked out but one such figure, Helen in the *Emperor and Galilean*, and he chastises her as only the world's greatest poets for the stage have dared to chastise her like before him. Through Ibsen, as through Shakespeare, we get a striking impression, that the one absolutely unpoetical thing in humanity is to be born to develop through struggle and change into a human being, and yet to will to have one's influence in life only as being a beautiful animal.

Other poets,—modern Frenchmen, and Swinburne even more than they,—may show by the strongest language, that they hold this same view, and how every such woman exists but as an injury, a sort of scar on humanity's living organism; but all their words only increase her power, and she knows this only too well.

Under our existing social conditions Silence is the only thing which can possibly lessen her death-bringing power;—that people should find a world-renowned poet, who knows how to touch all the fine chords of ideality, and at the same time is wide awake to all that goes on around him, simply sets her aside, wholly ignores her, or makes her a mere listener, puts her outside the real action of the poem, and in the same position as a listless and ignorant person occupies during brilliant conversation among intelligent people ; so that the reader or the onlooker is obliged to ask himself, how a being thus spiritually defective could ever have got a place amid the awakened life of human work and human will.

Thinking Frenchmen seem to wish to treat such women not as exceptions to womanhood, but as characteristic of it ; but whether the woman be cunning or simple, coquette or prude, she never arrives at any development through the action of the piece, and there is nothing to show whether she will end in being like her surroundings, or be educated by life into real womanhood. Ibsen, on the contrary, handles the question of development seriously, as being for woman the question of awakening in the end to being able to love devotedly and really.

It is not only as an idealist, that Ibsen knows this is the highest thing ; he knows as a realist, as a friend to the modern philosophy of development or 'evolution,' that every return to an earlier or ruder view of life, when a more human one has already entered the general consciousness, is unnatural. With these two convictions, he plans his work and carries it out ; he feels he is the messenger of nature and the spirit ; and therefore, amid the moral anachronisms in the rest of European poetry, he bursts in like a storm from the North to clear the air. So far as he is concerned, he will contribute nothing to justify antiquated habits of thought.

Ibsen considers that the womanly life which is available for dramatic purposes,—all the conditions for passionate action among woman's virtues and sins, together with the events arising out of them,—are different from what they were in past times, because the sort of influence it is now natural for her to strive after, is different.

Woman of course exercises influence in all possible ways ; but if it be not that of a free and loving being, it drags down ; it is an influence of somnambulism, death, and retrogression, a return to the Oriental idea of the relation between the sexes, according to which it is a merit for her to have no soul.

Against this now antiquated, animal view, whether on its respectable or its unrespectable side, Ibsen wages ceaseless war, and with a strategy that he has devised for himself. At any rate, he has turned his back on the French method which has been so industriously copied.

All women who willingly or unwillingly are part of the con-

indecency for maintaining the exclusive responsibility of man's qualities in the world, all women who thus consciously or unconsciously, are foes to woman's development, and, if they try to have influence, try to have it in some other, and therefore some unnatural way,—Ibsen disposes of summarily: in Princess Helen and a few others. And he considers he has then got rid of the whole brood.

But the richest streams from the royal veins of his poetry flow towards the other women, who are natural, fresh, self-deceived; who desired development, but did not, as a rule, find circumstances ripe enough to give it them; who were thus cheated out of life; who were alone in their day, or even before their day. He considers that he has a good opportunity for doing this, even when he is handling the great historic forces of the world, religious and other grave matters; his reason presumably being, that he considers these great things can never be settled without one half of the human race.

It is, then, marriage in its widest sense, the common work of man and woman, which is the question of questions to the great poet; the question which involves the final untying of every knot of difficulty, or at least the question whether or no we are to realise the idea of our race.

Nothing is justifiable in man or woman which is one-sided. Ibsen's plays show what ruin the Furies of one-sidedness can work, in the absence of harmonious understanding between man and woman. Ibsen views the relation between the sexes as the ultimate cause our reason can trace for all the unloveliness our race has inherited. This unloveliness may have more remote causes; and he suggests these infinite questions, but without believing he can get incontestable answers to them, as he believes he can about marriage.

A reader who from nature or teaching, inclines to the Oriental view of the sexes, will find Ibsen's writings merely 'destructive' and 'negative.' Our examination will lead us, however, to see, that his poetry is more constructive and positive than any other of his time; for to say that, for us human beings, a wrong relation between the sexes is the visible reason for all that is unlovely, is the same as saying, that beauty, or the realizing the idea of our race, is much nearer to us, more natural, more possible, than we could otherwise dare to believe.

The contempt for women associated with Don Juan's name has given place to another story, also a mediæval one, that of Venus and Tannhauser, where woman is the leader astray; and just now this is the only story which is applied in dramatic writing. Possibly some poets fancy that they do woman honour thereby, so far as her sex may be said to exercise a sort of right of chastisement for centuries of hampered development. The poison does not

B

consist in our awakening to the consciousness, that we ⬛
senses as well as souls. That consciousness is exactly what ⬛
should rouse and help to set in order; he is the only ⬛
really qualified to do it. The poison consists in getting ⬛
natural dislike at all lessened towards the Venus and Tannh⬛
story, and the representation of our nature underlying it, w⬛
meaning is a thousand times more lowering to all that wo⬛
means in this world, than any told of Don Juan. For when ⬛
story had done its worst, it had but expressed the dishono⬛
some one woman. The Venus story disgraces the whole sex, ⬛
does it through a woman.

And the most refined, surest, most weakening poison of ⬛l,
consists in regarding such scenes as living pictures, where ⬛
historical consequences of action appear, or rather no con⬛
quences of any sort; but where the events are a joke, and t⬛
end a joke, and the whole a mere amusement, a cannibal feast,
where the actresses are crowned with roses.

There is not a drop of this poison in Ibsen's poetry. Thi⬛
should not be forgotten, in reckoning up the essentials, whenev⬛
his title 'Woman's Poet' is in question; for there is no mistakin⬛
its meaning in an author so powerful as he is; it cannot aris⬛
from any want of power to choose or manage material. It mean⬛
neither more nor less than that Ibsen will not depict a woman,
using power, when this power is based on hampered development; he considers that idea has had its day, and must now be
consigned to the tomb; though in all his plays he allows for
difference of historical period, and for individual strength or
weakness.

~~Ibsen's women are generally beings with a power to accom-~~
~~plish an entire and distinct task in life, such women as, when~~
~~life at any time offers them a share in action, put their mask on~~
~~it, in the same way~~ as women like them will, when more sensible
manners shall prevail in the world, and earth's face grow young
once more, with springs of blessing which are now sealed up.
Even the wives who were not their husbands' choice, and therefore never had anything of a real wife's lot, even the disappointed
old maids or the spoilt girls, do their best in their distorted
position; when a moment for action or liberty comes, they show
that their heart is still in the right place, even though it be not a
wholly fresh, courageous heart.

And of the powerful women, who pioneer their own way, and
whose career is easier to follow, because it is more dramatic, it
may be said, that their very crime does but show the obverse side
of the devotedness which could have made them thorough women.

The strength of Ibsen's drawing of men's character has never
been questioned; men recognize past times and themselves through
them; nor can these impressions ever be forgotten. But these

......tly negative representations are not his most beautiful. His most beautiful things are his positive pictures of womanhood, and they only are (like Shakespeare's) clearly marked and completely carried out. The friendly, hopeful light they shed, only strikes our eyes, perhaps, when thrown into a strong contrast with the view man has hitherto held as to the position of the women. The poet has cut his way right through the thorny wood, to the dwelling where womanliness is to be found. After that, it depends upon each man, whether he will follow the path, and up to raise the newly-roused woman to full consciousness.

The end of the story of the sleeping wood Ibsen leaves to the reader. How he has carried it out, we know now; and how his own way is to show woman respect by his poetry; how cautious, how intensely modest he is, how manly his honesty is, how artistically chaste, how free from all sentimentality, all flowery language, all patronizing approval. Ibsen's method is not to get a chorus, but to secure silence and transparent air round his object. He wants, like a believer, rather to get to know something than to say something, when by one great poem after another he carefully opens the way to the fresh new forces in humanity: Woman.

Ibsen considers that it is from man's side that the greatest hindrances come to the realization of marriage on earth;—unity, positive purity, complete oneness of life and work between man and woman; but that woman increases man's difficulties in getting into the right way, because she does not understand his temptations, and has not learnt to cherish a noble respect for his fight.

Man has inherited more than woman has, of the disordered instincts which result from all false marriage, in countless previous generations. The physical and spiritual laws are yet unknown which enable heredity to give this different stamp to the two sexes, and thus a great difference in the difficulties of life's problems. How the matter actually stands is, on the contrary, plain to every one; and also that even the womanly woman will contribute to man's fall, while our present social ideas are in force. She does it from want of courage. But the results of an action may be equally great, whether it was intentional or unconscious. The momentary, unconscious crime is often a result of our not being developed enough to face the task from which we shrink. Whole hosts of such actions or omissions file through the world in silent darkness; and people who prefer that man should be left in his undeveloped condition, take pious comfort from thinking that these evils arise without any blame to the person who set them going. If only no one can be made personally responsible as the cause, they think the evils can be borne with meekness, and they accustom themselves to calling them 'natural' evils. No small part of the poet's task is to rouse men from this

opiate comfort. He does it, not by denying the existence of
these evils, but by painting them in all their far-reaching consequences, and making all men collectively responsible for them.
The poet, like the thinker, does not consider, that it is a part of
the world's scheme, that it is out of evil good should arise ; but
knows, that it is we ourselves who futilize our common life ; and
therefore he regards it as no crime to disturb us in our sleepy
or pious disregard of bad conditions and false views of life. He
sees that the struggle against evil is quite serious enough, without
our refusing our support to good, by retaining habits which unconsciously and irresponsibly work evil. He believes, in short, that
the full development of all healthy forces can only lead to good.

The trivial social view against which Ibsen protests is, that for
two to become one and blessed is a mere dream, but that marriage
is something practical ; that while parents alone chose for their
children, marriage was on too narrow a basis, but that the happy
mean has been found, now the approval of all relatives and f
is sought. Against all such shallowness and cynicism,
protests, that human passions cannot be controlled by locks
opiates, and that the only possible help is for passion and
to go the same way.

There are two ways of working for reform : the politi
waits and steers his course ; the poet compromises nothing.
illustrate these two ways, let us take an example from the phys
world.

Human beauty is an exception, whereas it should be the r
People set to work to attack wrong clothing and food, bad ha
at home and at school. Doubtless all this is in the right directio
and some are convinced. But one day, by accident, one of th
who have listened and assented, opens a book of engravings fro
Greek sculpture, and seeing perfect beauty, he learns more fro
that single glance, than from all the indirect working of sanitar
teaching. He has seen what beauty looks like.

The poet's work gives a similar discovery of inner beauty or
moral life. Some of the clearest light Ibsen has so far shed on
marriage, we get from *Nora*. The problem is set in its purest
form ; no unfavourable circumstances hinder the working out of
marriage ; nor does the temper of Nora or Helmer ; both are
well fitted for married life, and everything points to their being
naturally suited to each other. The hindrance lies exclusively
in the application of a false view of life, or—if some insist it once
contained truth—a view which Western peoples have out-lived.
When Helmer said he would work night and day for his wife, his
were no empty words. He had done it, he meant to do it ; he
had been faithfully working for eight years, and there is no sign
that he meant to cease. His happiness lay in Nora's being
unruffled. Nor would he dream of curtailing what *he* considers

her wife's freedom, i. e. the happy play of her ~~imagination. He would deprive her but of one thing really. How could he claim to be a real man; he would say, if he~~ gave it to her? And he so far succeeds in unfitting her for action, that when she takes upon herself to meddle in realities, she immediately commits a crime! He gives her everything but his ~~confidence, just~~ because he has ~~anything to conceal, but happier~~ REASON.

~~Thousands who submit to society's usual~~ view of a right life between man and woman, express it by saying their home is 'like a doll's house'; others, more ~~serious, mean~~ that they ~~are~~ glad to see a woman cosy and ~~comfortable in this kind of cell.~~ Some ~~express themselves by saying,~~ "Helmer went too far; if he had given Nora a cookery-book instead of a tambourine all ~~would~~ have been well." Others say, "If Nora had but had a ~~sensible~~ woman for her friend, instead of that knitting book-~~keeping~~ Mrs. Linden, all would have gone smoothly, even the ~~scene with~~ Dr. Rank, which a little tact would have turned into ~~a charming concluding scene."~~

~~The~~ only reply to all these is to ask them to read *Nora* through ~~carefully~~ once more, when they will see for themselves all the ~~conditions~~ for a moral marriage laid down. They may be summed up in the one word, Love. But at present Love is an idea to which no clear meaning attaches. Love presumes youth as a rule, but is not the same thing as youth, or even as youth with warm and mutual liking into the bargain. Youth is a glorious thing, but it has its own dangers; and the chief of them is self-deception. ~~It is only too easy for two young people to rock themselves in dreams of bliss without real love, in which case all relation between them is according to~~ Western notions immoral,— a point to which marriage makes no difference whatever. ~~Love is confidence; and Mrs. Linden and Krogstad, shipwrecked folks, as they were, had better prospects of it in their union, than Nora and Helmer had, because they meant to live in future with mutual understanding.~~ For marriage is really a state of being awake to life and activity; at least nine-tenths of it is active; and every piece of activity from which either mate excludes the other, is a piece of robbery from the marriage winnings or the mutual development marriage is intended to bring about for both, and therefore for humanity; quite apart from whether the activity itself fails or succeeds. It will generally be found, that those who dislike *Nora* are those whose view of marriage the play utterly destroys; while those who like the play, are those who, with Ibsen himself, would rejoice with all their hearts, to see that poor ideal of marriage crushed, against which every word in *Nora* quietly strikes a certain death-blow.

If you lose sight of the play's great human interest, you come to petty considerations; such as whether Nora had a really large

nature and Helmer a stupid one ; or that Ibsen means very little
in it after all ; or as to the effect it is likely to have in making
foolish young people neglect their duties, and turn from Chris-
tianity to Nihilism.

A poetical work reveals an idea, a truth which has a perfect
right to its place among the truths of the world ; a truth which
is so permanent and indestructible, that if the time has come for
that truth, it cannot be injured by neglect, or evaded or turned
aside, though he who attempts to injure it, may thereby injure
and destroy himself. A perfect poem sets forth an idea perfectly.
Either *Nora* is not a poetical work, or at any rate not a perfect
one ; or else by means of the idea it sets forth, it is perfectly easy
to find our way into every corner of the play, and get a clearer
and deeper knowledge of it, than would be possible from, *e. g.* an
historical essay. On the other hand, with anything less than this
idea, it is impossible to do justice to the play as a whole, or to
any of its organic parts.

The idea in *Nora* is : the object of marriage is to make each
human personality free. However incontrovertible this may be
when laid down as an axiom, does that confer the power of giving
it expression in real life, steering one's way among all the difficulties of deceit, inexperience, etc. ? Doubtless not ; but the
poet's work tells us, that until the relation between man and
woman turns in this direction, the relation is not yet Love. This
is the idea in *Nora*, freed from all side issues, and no other key
will unlock it.

It is of course possible to find one's way through schematic
plays, products of a weaker time than ours, without grasping the
main idea. But in our realistic art, when people speak the
language of their own passions and prejudices, we could never
reach the main idea through the various details, in so many ways
may an individual utterance be taken. The poet does not
create ideas ; as a rule, he can hardly be said to discover them ;
in most cases, they have already become human property, as
it were, amongst a few of his most thoughtful and cultured
contemporaries. But it is the poet's art which brings them to
light ; he communicates them to millions. What is new seems
dumb, while its spokesmen are the philosophers, statesmen,
priests, moralists, critics, sociologists, or publicists. It is as
though unsaid, till the poet says it ; when he has spoken,
humanity has spoken ; the thought is born on the lips of all, and
it is for the simple reason, that he cannot give it complete utterance until the hour has struck, and humanity has got so far, that
the new thing is said from necessity.

Some people consider that *Nora* shows the exaggeration of
genius, and not the beautiful, balanced revelation of a newly-
reached awakenedness in our moral conscience ; others admit that

the Oriental ideal of marriage must be given up, but ask why Nora
ends with a breaking off, and not a warning? Nora's own words
to Helmer give the answer; but she speaks so like and so unlike
the old morally unconscious being, whose development we have
been following step by step, that we are unwilling to recognise her
words in their full meaning. Perhaps it could be philosophically
demonstrated, that to say this does her great injustice, the same
injustice as she complains her father and husband did her; no
one will ever begin to treat her as a human being; no one shows
honour for her real respect for her own responsibility, and she
has the same right to it as a man has. Perhaps all this could be
proved, but feeling it only convinced by feeling or by reality.

Let us then construct another ending to Nora. Let us suppose
that the doll's house does not fall to pieces, but that Helmer
keeps his old delusion as to Nora's being a weak creature. There
is no doubt, that he would act exactly as he spoke; he would
forgive her; and, since the time for education had begun, he
would be a most careful schoolmaster. Nora would take no step
without his help; she would be just as much tied and bound as
before, with no will or conscience of her own.

He says, "I have power to become another man." She
replies, "Yes, when your doll is taken from you." She is
probably right; but it is certain that unless it happens, this
loving husband, the faithful, and, as some would say, the
'morally' loving man, will never change, never for a moment
come near guessing what morality in love really is: the effort
to make the beloved one free, awakened, responsible, true, pure-
hearted, noble, and strong; instead of enslaving, and making the
beloved dependent, irresponsible, double, needing help, slavish-
minded, and clinging. Helmer,—who has such an intense wish
to be a patron, and has such an artificially developed gift for
patronizing,—must continue to believe he possesses at least one
being destined for liberty, conscientious life, and personality, as
his private slave, who is favoured by partiality, and shielded
wisely, tenderly, and chivalrously. He will be sure to go on in
the belief, that there is at least one fellow-creature, who has no
will but his, even if outside home's shelter he is often tried, as he
probably will be, by painful miscalculation in such matters; e. g.
if the Bank staff were to be ungrateful for his fostering care of
them, and his humane attempt to absorb their personality in his
own. The 'doll,' the dream-creature, to whom he gave Nora's
shape, is not to be taken from him; he is to be able to go on
hugging that untrue view of half-humanity to his broad breast,
just as a child hugs its doll. He is to suffer much, because he is
an intelligent and sensitive man, but he is not to suffer in that
way, by having his eyes opened to what Nora is: Woman, or
the woman who should have been the angel of freedom to him.

But if this constructed ending to the play be rejected, surely a
happy one of some sort could be found? A novelist's mouth
must be watering to make Helmer lose his money,—*e. g.* by
Krogstad working him out of the Bank,—and then Nora is to
work for him and win his love. But we know that Nora has not
this sort of ascendancy in development, nor can have, with the
education life has so far given her. Torvald's illness did not
reveal them to each other, nor did eight years' struggle with
poverty. Ibsen has intentionally barred that outlet for us. The
struggle would only set Nora's energy in motion, till she found
it was praised like a good child's task, but not with respect, not
with humanity's charter of freedom—open, high-minded, devoted
trust. When she saw that that 'miracle' did not come, she
would grow weary. And garlanded slavery under poverty's roof
would be no better, but rather worse, than it was under the roof
of prosperity.

In all trials common to both, Helmer would do his duty, pre-
serve his equilibrium, and remain just what he always was. For
he is a 'gentleman'; let us give him full credit for that; but he
is not a real man, and years would but mark this more clearly.
His principles would dry up into mere maxims, his duty, honour,
taste, and judgment into routine ; till he ended in being one of
those faultless persons, with whom no one would dream of ex-
changing ideas on any subject, great or small ; but who, on the
contrary, by tacit understanding, are listened to with a respectful
smile, when they are so obliging as to communicate any view they
happen to hold.

Some are ready to agree: "We never were deeply imbued
with belief in Mr. Helmer's ideality; but why did Nora run
away in such haste? We cannot see that she gained anything,
poor creature, or that her little children did, by losing her motherly
care." Let us see if we can justify the mistake with which they
thus charge Ibsen. Their words imply, that the story of the
forgery, the agony of mind during Christmas week, the explanation between husband and wife, were a mere accidental dis-
turbance ; that in a week it would all be forgotten, as Helmer
says, and buried in a month or two. At first, no doubt, Nora
would be merrier and more docile than ever, and Helmer fonder
of his wife than even in the days when their home-life first began.
But as the weeks went by, Nora would be neither her present
nor her former self. As the memory of the great day faded, a
nervousness would creep over her, such as Helmer never dreamt
of. Either she would ask his opinion every other minute, evidently
to get rid of some secret restlessness; or without asking it, she
would be found undertaking things which in the old fonder days,
it would never have occurred to her to attempt alone. And if
Helmer did not answer her questions, she would cry; and if he

quietly expressed his surprise at his wife's taking her own course, she would break out into wondering assertions, always ending with the one which decided him to despatch Krogstad's dismissal : that he is petty.

Helmer would now begin to find it is high time to fulfil his promise of leaving the stage of play, and devoting himself to that of education. He adds that occupation to all his others, in an orderly way, and with the great power of getting through work which we know him to possess. He would try first one thing and then another. That Mrs. Krogstad is not the most suitable companion for Nora, would be his earliest discovery in his work of reformation. Result : Nora sometimes really avoids Christina, at others—as often as possible—contrives to meet her without Torvald's knowing it. She wants to tell her daily hopes and troubles to the industrious, sympathetic woman who was her friend in childhood; and all the time she contrives to appear to her husband as desiring no society but his. The attempt to be Will and Conscience to another shows its usual results : deception, hypocrisy, crooked ways, duplicity, loss of trust, absence of ease, joy, and healthiness in daily intercourse, and a habit, which seems to have taken root very quickly, of covering the abyss with artificial liveliness.

Let us suppose, however, that Helmer makes himself into a domestic school inspector of Nora's ways with the children, and points out, that if she is to do her duty by them and have time for him too, she must shop less, and spend less time with her dressmaker. Nora would try; but some day or other, in the middle of one of his nursery inspections, questions would burst from her lips, such as, *What* is skill with children ? *How* much 'self-control' and 'method' is to be expected from them, without sacrificing their individuality? and, *What* things ought one to pretend not to see ?

Helmer wonders when his discoveries in this strange woman's nature will come to an end, and where she can have got this new barrier from, which hinders husband and wife from their common work.

Such signs of self-guidance touch the most sensitive point in his view of life, as they always have done. We can hear him say, as he did once before, "Now we'll put an end to this, once and for all."

He is not eager about it ; he wishes to spare her, so far as possible. He says little ; but what he does say, so oppresses Nora, that she loses what little pleasure she ever took in the development of Ivar, Bob, and Emmy. But when a person like Nora once gets frightened, there is an element of rebellion in it ; feeling in the dark as she is after self-dependence, when she may not create something, she must at least destroy. So at one time,

she is cold and dull with the children; at another, she spoils
them, and fills their heads with the idea they ' must not tell papa.'
The new dominion over her Conscience and Will has only led
her to fresh lies; it has only dragged her deeper into the mud,
and this time, it is the children's turn to go with her and get
soiled. Thus Boredom will settle down on that home, as on
thousands of other homes. But that was not the air which was
wafted towards us, when the curtain first rose. The air was
restless perhaps, but one felt there were possibilities.

Is Helmer a bad man, then; coarse, dilatory, or boisterous
and domineering at times? No, he is quoted everywhere as a
model husband, and not without reason. He is merely colour-
blind in one direction, educated into colour-blindness.

One thing is certain; amid all this new order of things, he
yearns for the lark and the squirrel, the careless gaiety of the
Nora that used to be, and that is sometimes now when she
makes an effort. Then it strikes him, that it is unnatural to shut
up a young and beautiful woman; so he takes her into society,
to obliterate the past which perhaps preys on her mind, and to
' draw out the child in her nature.' For wise men think a
woman never grows; or that it is happier for her not to grow;
and that she can be stunted in her growth, as it used to be
thought puppies could by brandy.

A glance around us shows us many women arrested thus, many
rich young souls prevented from ever becoming real women.
It is a social murder, whose results are most disastrous for human
destiny. It means that homes can get amiable hostesses without
husbands getting loving wives, or children loving mothers. Will
this succeed in Nora's case? She is not a doll; but will Society's
stupefying agencies make her into one,—a model doll, a splendid
example of self-satisfied, undeveloped humanity, who will be
described as perfectly *comme il faut?*

Readers who desire this say, " We cannot see into each others'
hearts, and Nora's inner life may be anything she pleases; but
a well-bred woman should always seem at ease, and make it
possible for us to have dealings with her." Nora will never
come up to their expectations. There is something untamed in
her, which will make her sin continually against worldly rules. She
might dress as becomingly as any one, but there her likeness to
others would end. She does not belong to the class of women
whose two sections are the coquette and the prude, both being
the Doll grown to full stature. Such women are her only
enemies. They can lay aside conscience and ideality, without
loss of charm; they can never be free, nor make others free, never
love. They point in the opposite direction—to rule and be ruled;
they use freedom's means in the service of slavery. It is useless
to expect this of Nora. Her power of freedom, her need to love

and live really, are too strong to allow it, and will lead her to
break up life again and again, if Helmer continues unawakened
from his idea that conscience, will, personality, development and
human dignity are notions which concern men only, and this not
for himself alone, but for women as represented by him.

The associates Helmer would summon to help him in drawing
out Nora by 'society,' would find their pupil too hard to manage,
too individual, too inscrutable for them. She would win no
friends among women of the world. And although she is one
of those to whom men feel drawn, she will never secure one
thorough friend among them ; nor does she wish it, since she
found out Dr. Rank thought she had been making advances to
him. She will behave in a strikingly unsuitable manner in
society ; either too full of herself, or too indifferent. In either
case, she will wound Helmer's fine sense of what is fitting.
Sometimes, she will show unrestrained feeling, as she did in the
Tarantella, because she is secretly worried about something ; at
other times, she will take no interest in what is going on around
her. And if anybody in society turns specially to her, as though
to draw a little nearer to her real self, nothing will be got out of
her, except some utterly unsuitable answer ; an answer to the
thing, instead of an answer conveying an agreeable recognition
of the questioner's polite attention.

So Nora will get no recompense in society for her losses
at home—her husband's growing precision, or the children's
mixture of affection and disrespect, when at one time, she is
able to give them what they want behind their father's back,
and at another, cannot do what she promised them.

A few glimpses of happiness for Nora, and a sort of sad rest
for Helmer, may, however, come into their ruined home ; not
when the family is alone, for then the tension is only too plain ;
but when they give small parties, and the hostess is able to lay
down her own rules for etiquette, and charms herself into a
fancied self-guidance and liberty, for a few hours. Young people
will feel particularly happy on these occasions ; and Nora will
flash out for a few moments and seem young again. When all
this is over, Torvald, who is still in love with her, will spend
long hours in painfully pondering what it *is* that he has done,
that his young, happy, warm world has been cut away from
under him ; that he, though he has continued master in his own
home, really *has* no home now ?

Need we follow them further ?—into the critical years, when the
absence of ideality has made them grotesque ; when young people
laugh in Helmer's face at his way of playing *le père noble* ;
when Nora is middle-aged ; and some chance opening of the box,
where a pair of silk stockings has lain 'ever since that night,'
tempts from mamma's lips, a neat little description of her triumphs

at the costume ball, ending with the remark that Emmy has her
mother's foot and ankle, but she " must not think of putting on
that charming dress and dancing with the tambourine, poor little
Emmy ! or let out that she has ever seen them ; papa can't bear
such things, you know."

Such, then, is that to which in the most favourable circumstances, a mere ' warning' must have brought Nora and Helmer,
being what they were by nature and education.   We should see
Nora selfish, but with the selfishness which is more or less in
every natural woman's heart ; which unchecked and suppressed,
destroys either her whole woman's personality, or the happiness
and honour of all around her ; but raised to the moral plane of
freedom, would, on the contrary, have saved both. And we should
see Helmer selfish ; in a certain sense, more so than Nora ; but
selfish with the egoism of his sex, with satisfaction that he is a
man, and not a woman, rather than with any very exaggerated
individual egoism.   He is typical of the class of men on whom
the punishment falls most heavily of women not getting a true
human education, but being brought up to self-deception instead ;
and it is rather the punishment of his whole sex which he bears
than any tragic fate of his own, in bearing the consequences of
not having promoted his wife's human development.

Let us now see what prospect there is of reconciliation between
the Adam and Eve, whom Ibsen drives out of their Paradise
into the world of consciousness.   Everything in the play
strengthens our perception of the bare truth, that these two
people have by their life together, brought matters to such a pass,
that before anything good can come to them, Helmer must try
to come to himself, and Nora to herself. And at the last moment,
there seems a prospect, that they will achieve it some day. And
earthly life offers no truer ground for reconciliation than this, if
we believe development to be the end of our existence.   Every
right-thinking person must feel compelled to admit, that Nora's
fight for existence, as it faces her in all its cruelty, deserves our
love a thousand times more than any return to the Doll's House
conditions of ruining herself, her husband, and her children ; but
this by no means prevents his feeling painfully affected by the
idea of Helmer's petted wife, Ivar's, Bob's, and Emmy's merry
little mother, going away and shutting the door between herself
and them.   It is the only violent action in the last scene, and it
makes us feel all the indescribable pain which must weigh on that
undeveloped, newly-roused being, on the threshold between her
past and her future.

What is the outlook for him who is left behind on the stage ;
between his certainty of crushed happiness, and the hope of
higher things arising?   He thought himself so pure-hearted and
justifiable in everything ; he finds he only possessed a favourite

slave. Is it only mechanically that he repeats her words, 'the greatest miracle,' or does a new hope arise within him? The poet bids us think he has some new hope. Is it that Nora will repent and return? Her love needs no such change; she expects a real change in him. Through all the mist of his errors and projections, has he not caught a glimpse of the real Nora, the higher Eros, whom Socrates calls the oldest of all the gods; and, bowed to the earth with blushes, yet thankful he has learnt to blush, does he not say to himself, "A woman, too, is intended to be a human being"? Then he asks, "Am I a human being? Have I not made a slave of her, who might have helped me to freedom?"

How near to freedom he is, no one can determine, not even the poet himself; because the path to freedom is one which cannot be marked out beforehand. But everything in the play indicates that he will attain it. And if he does, it will be no small matter, that in everything but what concerned Nora, he was an honest man.

Since the idea in *Nora* is plain to all, we will now inquire what means Ibsen selected from every-day life, to make his meaning clear. The kernel of every home is its womanly principle; and the kernel of Ibsen's play is Nora's character. He means to make a modern home go to pieces before our very eyes, from some necessity within itself. It must contain everything that can attract: simplicity, gladness, power of work, good temper, gentle and strong regard, love of beauty, merry little children, friends, well-managed servants, good habits, good reputation, a position which has at length been won by praise-worthy endeavours, etc.; but also a husband who has such an essentially false idea of happiness between man and woman, that it has practically undermined this delightful home, and it is ready to fall in, at any moment.

The husband, too, is such a pleasant man, that his Oriental view of woman is ennobled, so far as a view can be, which is so inhuman and wounding to us. His belief, not that humanity is creation's king, but that man is, comes out in a kind, quiet way; if ever otherwise, he soon recovers his Oriental manly dignity, as though to say: "I forgot myself. I judged her as though she were a human being. In my haste, I overlooked the fact of her being only a woman. But it shall not happen twice. Henceforth I will abide faithfully and true to my principle that I, and I only, bear the burden and responsibility for us both."

If these presumptions are sufficiently unmistakable at every turn in the play, the spectator knows from the very beginning, that some of the indispensable conditions for healthy develop-

ment are wanting, and that the breaking up of the Doll's House
is only a question of time.

But it might have lasted a lifetime, as so many false marriages
do; and in that case, it would not have been a suitable subject
for a play. The dramatist did not need for his object a strong
character, such as could have set the wrong right, and kept the
home together; or a 'passive' woman, whose will is dead; or
one with 'a broken heart'; or a superficial person, who ends
in being satisfied with trifles; or one who suffers, and weeps, and
sighs; or one of those, who combine any of these characters with
that of a prude or a coquette. Any one of these women would
have delayed the climax, so as to destroy dramatic possibilities;
nor would a large and highly religious womanly figure have
been suitable; still less would one already exhausted by homage
to propriety and custom.

They needed a young creature, loving but undisciplined; full
of life, but lacking all principle in thought and action; blind
to all but what is nearest at hand, but ready to love with her
whole strength, that is, to devote all her happiness to what is
nearest her; otherwise, cruel with indifferent carelessness, but
only because no notion of the rights of others, of 'strangers,'
has ever been presented to her; capable as a child of nature is, of
stealing on behalf of her own dear ones, but not capable as an
artificialized nature is, of stealing from them in order to gratify her
private vanity before strangers with what she has thus stolen;
gentle to those nearest her, but not to others or to herself;
an uneducated girl, who never had a mother; one who, as a
daughter and a growing girl, had to get what poor little exchange
of thought she could in the maids' room; a wife who is obliged
to choose as her confidential friend her husband's friend, and not
her husband himself; a beautiful, attractive young woman, who
feels she is independent, placed in the high position of head
of a house, but who, none the less, has come to tricking her
husband, by lie after lie in daily life; half-consciously longing,
and waiting outside in the darkness, for some change which is to
come suddenly, 'the miracle,' she does not exactly know what;
but its effect is to be that the activity of her soul and her husband's are no longer to be *allowed* to go different ways; that
what *she* tries, what *she* accomplishes, what *she* sacrifices, is to
be reckoned as human, like his. The poet must find all these
elements, like mines ready laid, in the woman's character, upon
which the existence of the home is based. No one of them must
fail him, when the match is put to the train, if the Doll's House
is to be blown to unrecognizable pieces before our eyes.

Nora is precisely all this. The poet has now what he wants;
it is as in real life: the persons of the action have no notion
what they are about, until the moment of parting.

When all is falling to pieces, and not a ▓▓▓▓ sooner, they see by a sudden flash, how they have been gradually bringing their fate on themselves, as ▓▓▓▓▓▓▓▓▓▓▓▓▓▓▓ full life: the ▓▓▓, by not having considered the woman's personality; the woman, by ▓▓ ▓▓▓ having loved a ▓▓▓▓ who ▓▓▓ ▓▓▓▓▓▓ whoever the more unfortunate in her own ▓▓▓ turned her best deeds into faults.

It has been alleged, that Nora is not the same person in her concluding scene with Helmer as she is throughout the play. So far as her understanding goes, she is just the same. Her one reproach to Helmer at the end is, that he did not take the blame on himself; and her calm at the end is so touching, because the spectator knows what Helmer neither knows nor believes, that she was really ready to die to save him from the necessity of taking the blame on himself. For she means it in perfect good faith; in a few minutes she will jump into 'the cold black water,' which does not, however, prevent her,—with her childish optimism, her habit of succeeding, and her power of telling herself tales (such as of the old gentleman who was to leave her his property), —having some hope that the water might not be cold, or not drown her, or might change her into some new being, whom no anxiety could threaten. For even in this last and most honest resolve to die, she is not acting as one fully awake, responsible, and conscious. She is all this for the first time, at the moment she breaks away from Helmer and goes. But it is the old Nora; only it is Nora on her most serious side; it is the young and inexperienced woman who, after Helmer's proper little speech gives her the experience which puts an end to her youth, cannot help telling him how boundlessly she once believed in him.

The same objection is urged by those who may, that she utters a number of incontestable truths, or, as her enemies describe it, 'makes a speech' at the end and 'preaches the doctrine of the future.' This, were it true, would prove her to be another Nora. But she really speaks as she always has spoken, without any calculation whatever. It is but the outburst of human nature's own consciousness of itself, but it has been so very recently awakened in her. It first awoke in her, at the moment when she finally discovered the thing, whose pain wrung from her . . . "It became clear to me that I had been living here all these years, with a strange man, and had borne him three children. Oh! I cannot bear to think of it! I could tear myself in pieces!"

Till then, she had never guessed, that her husband's Oriental view of life's task as adjusted to the two sexes had been a serious one, which had reduced her to a mere Thing, day after day—the dearest thing in all the world, but not a human being, not his peer. The moment she not only guessed this, but knew it with the most deadly cold certainty, every spark of womanly instinct told her, in that second, all that can ever be taught or known about it.

Nora herself is the Chorus to all the previous action, through the general truths she finally utters; but it is precisely because she only gets to know them at the very moment she utters them. It is just on such occasions as this, that people do speak, unless feeling chokes their words.

Nora's being able to speak harmonizes with her whole self. Helmer has always been mistaken in his notion that she was 'weak'; it was part of his false theory of a wife. She is rather strong than not, as appears in all her doings. And if women in general come to act more, the same thing will cause surprise in countless cases. Weakness is most often, nothing but destroyed power of thinking and doing. It is because her character is so capable of strong devotion that she can go away, when she finds she would do harm by staying; and can speak out all the hard new truths, feeling as she does, that she is no more fit to stay and educate him into them, than he is to educate her.

But people shoot beside the mark, too, when they will not see the subject of *Nora* as one of universal human application, when they think that Ibsen wanted to make Helmer hateful. What Ibsen wanted to make hateful, and what he has made hateful, is Helmer's false view of half humanity,—a view that still is the view of life which most men hold, and which makes it possible for a man to be every inch a gentleman, without being for that reason a human being; to believe he loves a woman, and at the same time think he can be Will and Conscience for her; which makes it possible for a woman to call these habits of thought in men Chivalry, and exercise every quality of her inner and outward being, only to secure the small triumphs of an odalisk; while at the same time she believes herself a pure-hearted woman, believes that she loves, believes that she really *lives*.

It is this social pest, this expression of what is unnatural, that Ibsen hates. For it is unnatural, standing as it does side by side with such a highly-developed notion of individuality as that now current in society. And Ibsen hates this, not because he delights to hate, but because, as a poet, he loves individuality with all his heart, and womanly individuality above all, as the friendly, dawning promise for all our retarded human development, as the most promising side in the gospel of Man, as the daylight side of the future.

FRANCES LORD.

London, November, 1882.

NORA.

(A DOLL'S HOUSE.)

PERSONS IN THE PLAY.

HELMER (*a lawyer*).
NORA (*his wife*).
DOCTOR RANK.
MRS. LINDEN.
KROGSTAD (*a business man*).
THE HELMERS' *three little* CHILDREN.
MARY ANN (*their nurse*).
A Maidservant *at the Helmers'*.
A Porter.
(*The action takes place at the Helmers' house.*)

ACT I.

*A room furnished comfortably and tastefully, but
not expensively.*

(*To the right, a door leads to the Hall; to the left,
another door in the background, to* Helmer's *study.
Between the two doors, a pianoforte.*

*In the middle of the left wall, a door, and some-
what nearer the front, a window. Near the window,
a round table with an arm chair and a small sofa.
On the right wall, somewhat to the back, a door. In
the same wall, more forward, a stove of porcelain;*

11

by it, a couple of arm-chairs and a rocking-chair. Between the stove and the side door, a small table. Engravings on the walls. An étagère with china and other small curiosities. A small book-case of showily-bound books. Carpet. A fire burns in the stove. It is winter.)

(The bell rings in the hall outside. Presently, the hall door is heard opened. Nora walks into the room, humming contentedly. She is in walking dress, and has several parcels in her arms, which she lays on the right-hand table. She leaves the door into the hall open behind her, and a Porter is seen standing outside, carrying a Christmas tree and a basket; he gives these to the Maidservant, who opened the door.)

NORA. Be sure you hide the Christmas tree most carefully, Ellen ; so that the children don't catch sight of it, on any account, before this evening, when it is dressed and lit. *(To the Porter, taking out her purse.)* How much?

PORTER. Sixpence, if you please, ma'am.

NORA. There is a shilling . . . No, keep the change.

(The Porter thanks her and goes. Nora shuts the door. She continues smiling with quiet contentment, while she is taking off her walking things. Then she takes a box of maccaroons from her pocket, and eats some. As she does so, she steps cautiously to her husband's door and listens.) Yes ; he is at home. *(She begins humming again, walking to the right-hand table.)*

HELMER *(in his room).* Is that my lark, who is twittering outside there?

NORA (*busy opening some of her parcels*). Yes, it is.

HELMER. Is it the little squirrel running about?

NORA. Yes.

HELMER. When did it get home?

NORA. Just this minute. (*Hides the box of maccaroons in her pocket, and wipes her mouth.*) Come in here, Torvald, and see what I have bought.

HELMER. I can't be interrupted now. (*A little later he opens the door and looks in, pen in hand.*) 'Bought,' did you say? What! all that heap of things? Has my little spendthrift bird been wasting more money?

NORA. But, Torvald, we really can be a little less strict now. It is positively the first Christmas we aren't obliged to pinch.

HELMER. Yes; but I'll tell you what: we mustn't waste money, either.

NORA. Oh, yes! Torvald, we may venture to spend a little already, mayn't we? just a very, very little. You have really got a capital position, and you'll be earning ever so much money.

HELMER. Yes, from New Year's Day. But there is a whole quarter before my next salary is due.

NORA. Never mind; we can <u>borrow</u> for that little time.

HELMER. Nora! (*He steps towards her and takes her playfully by the ear.*) Is that light-mindedness of yours coming out again? Supposing that I borrowed fifty pounds to-day, and you spent it during Christmas week, and that on New Year's Day a tile blew off the roof and struck my head, and I were . . .

NORA (*stopping his mouth*). Stuff! How can you say such horrid things!

HELMER. But, suppose anything of the kind were to happen. What then?

NORA. If such a misfortune were to happen, I should not care whether I had debts or whether I hadn't.

HELMER. But what about the people I had borrowed from?

NORA. Those people! Who would trouble about them? They would be strangers, of course.

HELMER. Nora, Nora! you are a mere baby. But seriously, Nora, you know my way of thinking about such matters. No debts! Never borrow! Home life ceases to be free and beautiful, directly its foundations are Borrowing and Debts. We two have held out bravely till now, and we will do so, for the little time now remaining.

NORA (*going to the fireplace*). Ye—s. Just as you like, Torvald.

HELMER (*following her*). Come, come; my lark must not let her wings droop immediately . . . What! is the squirrel making wry faces? (*Takes out his purse.*) Nora, what do you think I've got here?

NORA (*turning round quickly*). Money!

HELMER. There! (*Gives her some notes.*) By Jove! don't I know that all sorts of things are wanted at Christmas?

NORA (*counting*). Ten, twenty, thirty, forty. Oh! thank you, thank you, Torvald. This will help me on for a long while to come.

HELMER. That is just what it must do.

NORA. Yes, indeed, it will. But now you must come, too, and see all I have been buying. And so cheap! Look, here is a new suit for Ivar, and a little sword as well. Here are a little horse and a trumpet for Bob. And here are a doll and a cradle for Emmy. They are only common; but she would be sure to pull them all to pieces directly. And here I've got dresses and handkerchiefs for Ellen and Mary Ann. Only I ought to have got something better for Mary Ann.

HELMER. And what is that, in the other parcel?

NORA (*crying out*). No, Torvald, you're not to see that before this evening.

HELMER. Oh! ah. But now tell me, you little spendthrift, what you have got for yourself.

NORA. Never mind me. I don't want anything for myself.

HELMER. But I am sure you do. Just tell me something sensible you would like to have.

NORA. No; I really know of nothing . . . Yes; listen, Torvald.

HELMER. Well?

NORA (*playing with his coat buttons, without looking him in the face*). If you want to give me something, you might, you know, you might . . .

HELMER. Well, well? Out with it!

NORA (*quickly*). You might give me the money, Torvald. Only just as much as you think you can spare; then I will buy myself something with it, later on.

HELMER. But, Nora . . .

NORA. Oh, please do, dear Torvald, I beg and implore you. Then I would hang the money in lovely gilt paper, on the Christmas tree. Wouldn't that be funny?

HELMER. What do people call the bird who always spends everything?

NORA. Yes, I know: a spendthrift, of course. But please do what I ask you, Torvald. Then I shall have time to think what I most want. Is not that very sensible? Come!

HELMER (*smiling*). Certainly; that is to say, it would be if you really kept the money I gave you, and really bought yourself something with it. But it all goes in housekeeping, and for all sorts of useless things, and then I have to find more.

NORA. But, Torvald . . .

HELMER. Can you deny it, Nora dear? (*He puts his arm round her.*) My lark is the dearest little thing in the world; but she needs a very great deal of money. No one would believe how expensive such a little bird is for her husband to keep.

NORA. Rubbish! how can you talk so? I am sure I am as careful as I can be.

HELMER (*smiling*). Very true,—as careful as you can be. But you can't be careful at all.

NORA (*hums and smiles in quiet satisfaction*). Hm—m. You should just know, Torvald, what expenses we larks and squirrels have.

HELMER. What an odd little woman you are! Just like your father—always eager to get hold of money. But the moment you have it, it seems to slip through

your fingers somehow; you never know how you
got rid of it. Well, one must take you as you are.
It's in the blood. Yes, my dear Nora, you may
say what you please, but things of that sort are
inheritable.

NORA. Ah! there are many things I wish I had
inherited from father.

HELMER. And I couldn't wish you to be anything
but exactly what you are—my own, sweet, little lark.
But ... I say ... it strikes me ... you look so, so—
what shall I call it?—to-day ... as if you were hiding
something.

NORA. Do I?

HELMER. Yes, really. Look me full in the face.

NORA (*looking at him*). Well?

HELMER (*threatening with his finger*). That little
mouth, which is so fond of sugar-plums, has never
been eating any quantity of them, in the town,
surely?

NORA. No! How can you think anything of the
kind about me?

HELMER. Didn't the dainty-loving little person just
steal off to the confectioner's?

NORA. No, I assure you, Torvald ...

HELMER. Not to taste a few sweetmeats?

NORA. No; most certainly not.

HELMER. Not so much as to nibble a maccaroon
or two?

NORA. No, Torvald, I really do assure you. ...

HELMER. Well, well, well; of course I'm only
joking.

NORA (*goes to the right-hand table*). I should not think of doing what you disapprove of.

HELMER. I know, dear; and you have given me your word. (*Steps to her.*) No; keep your little Christmas secrets all to yourself, Nora dear. I have no doubt they will come to light this evening, when the Christmas tree is lit.

NORA. Have you remembered to invite Doctor Rank?

HELMER. No. But that is not necessary; it is an understood thing, that he dines with us. Besides, I shall tell him, when he looks in to-day. I have ordered some capital wine. Nora, you cannot think how I look forward to this evening!

NORA. So do I. And how happy the children will be, Torvald!

HELMER. Oh! it really is glorious to know, that one has got a safe and assured position, and has ample means. Isn't the consciousness of it a great enjoyment?

NORA. Oh! it is a miracle.

HELMER. Do you recollect last Christmas? Three whole weeks beforehand, you used to shut yourself up till long past midnight, in order to make flowers to trim the Christmas tree, and get ready all the other magnificent things to surprise us with. It was the most wearisome time I ever lived through.

NORA. It did not weary me at all.

HELMER (*smiling*). We did not see much for your pains.

NORA. Oh! will you never leave off teasing me

about *that!* How could I help it, if the cat did get in and tear everything I had made to pieces?

HELMER. To be sure, you couldn't help it, my poor little Nora. You set to work to prepare us a treat with the best will in the world, and that is the chief matter.... But, nevertheless, it is a good thing, that hard times are over.

NORA. Yes, it is exactly like a miracle.

HELMER. Now I needn't sit here all by myself, getting more bored every minute; and you needn't torment your blessed eyes and your delicate little fingers....

NORA (*clapping her hands*). It is really true, isn't it, Torvald, that we needn't do it any more? Oh! how splendid! (*Takes his arm.*) And now I will tell you, Torvald, how it has been striking me we ought to arrange matters.... Directly Christmas is over... (*The hall-door bell rings.*) Oh, there's a ring! (*She tidies the room a little.*) That is somebody come to call. How vexing!

HELMER. I am 'not at home' to callers. Don't forget that.

ELLEN (*in the doorway to* Nora). A strange lady wishes to see you, ma'am.

NORA. Show her in.

ELLEN (*to* Helmer). And the Doctor came at the same time, sir.

HELMER. Did he go straight into my study?

ELLEN. Yes, sir. (Helmer *goes into his study.* Ellen *shows in* Mrs. Linden, *in travelling costume, and shuts the door behind her.*)

MRS. LINDEN (*sorrowful and a little doubtful of a welcome*). How do you do, Nora?

NORA (*uncertain who she is*). How do you do?

MRS. LINDEN. I dare say you do not know me again.

NORA. No, I really. . . oh, yes—I think . . . (*Breaking forth*) What! Christina! Is it really you?

MRS. LINDEN. Yes; it is I indeed.

NORA. Christina! and to think I did not recognize you! But how could I even— (*More softly*) How altered you are, Christina!

MRS. LINDEN. Why! of course I am, in nine or ten long years.

NORA. Is it so long since we met? Yes, it positively is. Oh! the last eight years have been a happy time, I can tell you. And now you have come to town? all this long journey in mid-winter! That was brave of you.

MRS. LINDEN. I arrived by the steamer this morning.

NORA. In order to have some fun at Christmas time, to be sure. Oh, how delightful that is! Yes, fun we certainly will have. But take your things off. Aren't you frozen? (*Helps her to take her things off.*) There! now we will sit down here cosily by the fire. No; in that arm-chair; I will sit here in the rocking-chair. (*Takes her hands.*) Yes, now you are showing me your dear old face again. It was only the first moment I saw you. . . . But you are a little paler, Christina, and perhaps a shade thinner, too.

MRS. LINDEN. And much, much older, Nora.

NORA. Yes, perhaps a little older, too—a little wee bit, not much. (*She suddenly stops; seriously.*) Oh ! what a thoughtless creature I am ! Here I sit chattering on, and—Dear, good Christina, can you forgive me ?

MRS. LINDEN. What do you mean, Nora ?

NORA (*softly*). Poor Christina ! you are a widow.

MRS. LINDEN. Yes ; three years ago.

NORA. Ah ! I was sure of it. I read it in the newspaper, you know. Oh, do believe, Christina dear, I often meant to write to you then ; I was always planning to do it, but something always hindered me.

MRS. LINDEN. I can very well understand that, Nora dear.

NORA. No, Christina ; it was dreadful of me. Oh, you poor darling ! how much you must have gone through ! . . . And he really left you nothing in the world to live upon ?

MRS. LINDEN. No.

NORA. And no children either ?

MRS. LINDEN. No.

NORA. Then really nothing whatever ?

MRS. LINDEN. Not even a sorrow or a regret to waste my heart upon.

NORA (*looking at her incredulously*). But, my dear Christina, how is that possible ?

MRS. LINDEN (*smiling sadly and stroking her hair*). Oh, it happens so sometimes, Nora.

NORA. So utterly lonely !. . . How awfully hard that must be for you ! I have three of the dearest children that ever were. But I can't show them to you just now; they are out walking with nurse. However, now you must tell me your whole story.

MRS. LINDEN. No, no, I would rather hear yours.

NORA. No; you must begin; I won't be egotistical to-day. To-day I will think only of what concerns you. But one thing I really must tell you. Do you know what great good fortune has fallen to our lot in the last few days?

MRS. LINDEN. No. What is it?

NORA. Only think! My husband has been made Manager of the Joint Stock Bank.

MRS. LINDEN. Your husband! Oh, what a piece of luck!

NORA. Yes; tremendous, isn't it? A professional man's position is so uncertain, especially when he will not be concerned in any business except what is fit for a gentleman, and respectable. And naturally, Torvald would not do any other business; and in that matter I quite agreed with him. Oh! we are heartily glad, I can tell you. He will actually enter the Bank on New Year's Day, and then he will have a large salary, and high percentages on the business done. In future, we shall be able to live in a very different style from the way we have lived hitherto,—just as we please, in fact. Oh, Christina, I feel so light and happy . . . It really is beautiful, isn't it, to have a great deal of money, and be able to live without anxiety? Now isn't it?

MRS. LINDEN. Well; it cannot but be delightful to have bare necessaries.

NORA. No, not only bare necessaries, but a great deal of money—heaps!

MRS. LINDEN (*smiling*). Nora, Nora, haven't you grown sensible yet? In our school days, you were a great spendthrift.

NORA (*quietly smiling*). Yes; Torvald says I am so still. (*Threatens with her finger.*) But 'Nora, Nora,' is not so silly as you all think. Oh! our circumstances have really not been such that I could be a spendthrift. We both had to work.

MRS. LINDEN. You as well?

NORA. Yes, really;—light fancy work: knitting, crochet, and things of that sort (*as though throwing it away*), and also other work. I suppose you know, that when we married, Torvald quitted the Government service? He had no prospect of promotion in his office, and he certainly had to earn more money than before. I do assure you, that the first year he overworked himself quite terribly. You can easily understand, that he was naturally obliged to get all the extra work he could, and toil from morning till night. It was too much for him, and he fell dangerously ill. Then the doctors declared it was necessary for him to go to the South.

MRS. LINDEN. Yes; you spent a whole year in Italy, didn't you?

NORA. We did. It was not an easy matter to arrange, I can assure you. Ivar was only just born then. But we had to go. Oh, it was a wonderfully delicious journey! And it saved Torvald's life. But it cost an awful sum of money, Christina.

MRS. LINDEN. You needn't tell me that, dear.

NORA. Three hundred pounds. That's a great deal, isn't it?

MRS. LINDEN. But in such cases it is, after all, a most fortunate thing to have the money to spend.

NORA. Yes; I ought to tell you I got it from father.

MRS. LINDEN. Ah; I see. It was just about the time he died, I think?

NORA. Yes, Christina, just then. And think what it was for me not to be able to go to him and nurse him! I was expecting little Ivar's birth daily. And then I had my Torvald to nurse, who was dangerously ill too. Dear good father! I never saw him again, Christina. Oh! that is the hardest thing I have had to bear since I married.

MRS. LINDEN. I know you were devotedly fond of your father. And then you and your husband started for Italy?

NORA. Yes; by that time we had the money; and the doctors hurried us off. So we went a month after.

MRS. LINDEN. And your husband returned completely cured?

NORA. Sound as a bell.

MRS. LINDEN. But—the Doctor?

NORA. What about him?

MRS. LINDEN. I thought your servant said, that the gentleman, who came in just when I did, was the Doctor . . .

NORA. Yes, it was Doctor Rank. But he does not

pay any professional visits here. He is our best friend, and comes in to chat with us, at least once every day. No; Torvald has not had an hour's illness since we went to Italy. And the children, too, are so healthy and well, and so am I. (*Jumps up and claps her hands.*) Oh, dear! oh, dear! Christina, it is indeed wonderfully delicious to live and be happy!— Oh, but it is really horrible of me! I am talking about nothing but my own concerns. (*Sits down upon a footstool close to her, and lays her arms on Christina's knee.*) Oh! don't be angry with me for it. Now just tell me, is it really true, that you didn't love your husband? Why ever did you marry him, then?

MRS. LINDEN. My mother was living at that time, and she was bed-ridden and helpless; and then I had my two younger brothers to provide for. I did not consider I should be justified in refusing him.

NORA. Oh, yes. I dare say you were right there. Then he was rich in those days?

MRS. LINDEN. Very well off indeed, I believe. But his business was not sound, Nora. When he died, it all fell to pieces, and there was nothing left.

NORA. And then?

MRS. LINDEN. Then I had to try to make my way by keeping a small shop, a little school, and anything else I could get. The last three years have been for me one long working-day, without a moment's rest. But now it is over, Nora dear. My poor mother no longer needs me: she is at rest in her grave. Nor do the boys need me: they are in business, and can provide for themselves.

NORA. How relieved you must feel!

MRS. LINDEN. No, Nora: only inexpressibly empty. To have nobody you can devote your life to! (*Stands up, restless.*) That is why I could not bear to stay any longer, in that out-of-the-way little town. It must be easier to find something here, which really has a claim upon one and occupies one's thoughts. If I could but be so fortunate as to get a fixed post,—some office-work.

NORA. But, Christina, that is so terribly tiring, and you look so overdone already. It would be far better for you, if you could go to some cheerful watering-place for a while.

MRS. LINDEN (*going to the window*). I have no father who could give me the money to go, Nora.

NORA (*rising*). Oh! don't be vexed with me.

MRS. LINDEN (*going towards her*). Dear Nora, do not be vexed with me. The worst of a position like mine is, that it leaves the dregs of so much bitterness in one's mind. One has nobody to work for, and yet one is obliged to be always on the look-out for chances. Besides, one must live, and so one gets selfish. When you told me of the happy change in your circumstances,—you'll hardly believe it;—but I rejoiced more on my own account than on yours.

NORA. How do you mean? Ah! I see. You mean Torvald could do something for you.

MRS. LINDEN. Yes; I thought so.

NORA. And he shall, too, Christina dear. Just leave that to me. I shall lead up to it, in the most delicate manner in the world, and invent something plesesse, which he will thoroughly approve of. Oh I I should so like to be of some use to you.

MRS. LINDEN. How good of you, Nora, to take up my cause so zealously; it is doubly good in you, who know so little of the troubles and difficulties of life.

NORA. I? I know so little of—?

MRS. LINDEN (*smiling*). Bless me! a little fancy-work, and things of that sort. You are a mere baby, Nora.

NORA (*tosses her head and paces the room*). I would not be so positive, if I were you.

MRS. LINDEN. Really?

NORA. You are like everybody else. You none of you think that I could be of any real use. . . .

MRS. LINDEN. Come, come, darling—

NORA. —that I have had my share of difficulties in this troublesome world.

MRS. LINDEN. Dear Nora, you have just finished telling me the whole story of your trials.

NORA. I dare say—the little ones. (*Softly.*) The great thing I haven't told you about.

MRS. LINDEN. What great thing? What do you mean?

NORA. You overlook me so completely, Christina; but you ought not to do so. You are proud of having worked so hard and so long for your mother.

MRS. LINDEN. I am sure I ignore nobody. But it is true, I am proud and glad when I think, that it was my privilege to secure my mother the evening-time of her life tolerably free from care.

Nora. And you are also proud, when you think of what you did for your brothers.

Mrs. Linden. It seems to me, I have a right to be proud of it.

Nora. I quite agree. But now I will tell you something, Christina: I, too, have something to be proud and glad about.

Mrs. Linden. I don't doubt it. But what do you mean?

Nora. Not so loud. Suppose Torvald were to hear! He must not, for anything in the world. Nobody must get to know it, Christina; nobody but you.

Mrs. Linden. What can it be, my dear?

Nora. Come over here. (*Draws her down beside her on the sofa.*) Yes . . . I, too, have something to be proud and glad about. It was I who saved Torvald's life.

Mrs. Linden. Saved his life? How saved his life?

Nora. I told you about our Italian journey. Torvald could not have recovered, unless he had got down there.

Mrs. Linden. So I understood, dear; and your father gave you the needful money.

Nora (*smiling*). Yes; so Torvald and everybody else believes; but . . .

Mrs. Linden. But . . .

Nora. Father didn't give us one penny. It was I who found the money.

Mrs. Linden. You? The whole of that large sum?

NORA. Three hundred pounds. What do you say to that?

MRS. LINDEN. But, my dear Nora, how was it possible? Did you win it in some lottery?

NORA (*contemptuously*). In a lottery? Pooh! What would there have been clever in that?

MRS. LINDEN. Then wherever did you get it from?

NORA (*hums and smiles mysteriously*). Hm; tra-la-la-la !

MRS. LINDEN. For you certainly couldn't borrow it.

NORA. No? Why not?

MRS. LINDEN. Why! a wife cannot borrow without her husband's consent.

NORA (*throwing her head back*). Oh! when the wife is one who has some slight knowledge of business, a woman, who knows how to set about things with a little wisdom, then . . .

MRS. LINDEN. But, Nora, I can't in the least comprehend . . .

NORA. Nor need you, either. It has never been stated, that I borrowed the money. Perhaps I got it in another way. (*Throws herself back on the sofa.*) I may have got it from some ardent swain or another. When anybody is so distractingly pretty as I am . . .

MRS. LINDEN. You are a fool, Nora.

NORA. Now I am sure you are intensely curious, Christina . . .

MRS. LINDEN. Listen to me for a moment, Nora dear. Haven't you been a little indiscreet?

NORA (*sitting upright again*). Is it indiscreet to save one's husband's life?

MRS. LINDEN. It seems to me it was indiscreet, that you, without his knowledge . . .

NORA. But he mightn't know anything about it. Can't you comprehend that? He was not to guess, for a single moment, how dangerous his condition was. It was to me the doctors came, and said, that his life was in danger, that nothing could save him but living for a time in the South. Don't you suppose I should have tried to manage it in some other way, first? I laid before him how nice it would be for me, if I could have a journey abroad, like other young married ladies; I wept and prayed; I said he ought to consider my circumstances; and he might just as well be nice, and give me my own way; and then I hit upon the idea, that he could of course borrow the money. But when I said that, Christina, he got almost angry. He said I was giddy, and that it was his duty as a husband not to yield to my tempers and fancies,—yes, that was the word he used, I believe. 'Very well,' I thought; 'but saved your life must be;' and then I found a way to do it.

MRS. LINDEN. And did not your husband learn from your father, that the money was not from him?

NORA. No; never. Father died within those few days. I meant to have let him into my secret and begged him to tell nothing. But as he was so ill, . . unhappily it was not necessary.

MRS. LINDEN. And have you never since then, taken your husband into your confidence?

NORA. Dear me! What can you be thinking of? Tell him, when he is so strict on the point of not borrowing? And added to that, how painful and humiliating it would be for Torvald, with his man's idea of self reliance, to know that he owed anything to me. It would entirely upset the relation between us; our beautiful, happy home would never again be what it is now.

MRS. LINDEN. Will you never tell him?

NORA (*thoughtfully, half-smiling*). Yes,—later on perhaps,—after many years, when I have ceased to be so pretty as I am now. You mustn't laugh at me. Of course I mean, when Torvald is not so fond of me as he is now; when he no longer gets any amusement out of seeing me skipping about, and dressing up and acting. Then it might be rather a good plan to have something in the background. (*Breaking off.*) What nonsense! That time will never come. Now, what do you say to my grand secret, Christina? Am I not of some real use? Moreover, you will believe me when I say, the affair gave me much anxiety. It certainly has not been easy for me to meet my engagements punctually. You must know, Christina, that in the world of business, there is something which is called quarterly interest, and something which is called paying off by instalments; and they are so terribly hard to tide over. That compelled me to pinch a little, here and there, wherever I could. I could not lay anything aside out of the housekeeping money, for of course Torvald had to live well. Nor could I let the children go about badly dressed. All I received for that purpose I considered I ought to expend on it. The dear, darling children!

MRS. LINDEN. And so your own personal expenses had to be restricted? Poor Nora!

NORA. Yes, of course. I was the person on whom it bore heaviest. Whenever Torvald gave me money for clothes and similar things, I never used more than half of it; I always bought the plainest and cheapest kinds. It is most fortunate, that everything suits me so well; so Torvald never noticed it. But it was often very hard, Christina dear. For it really is very nice to be beautifully dressed. Now, isn't it?

MRS. LINDEN. I should think so, indeed!

NORA. Well, and besides that, I had other sources of income. Last winter, for instance, I was so lucky as to get a heap of copying work to do. Then I used to shut myself up every evening and write far on into the night. Oh, sometimes I was so tired, so dreadfully tired. And yet it was intensely amusing, nevertheless, to sit working in that way and earn money; I almost felt as if I were a man.

MRS. LINDEN. But how much have you been able to pay off in this way?

NORA. Well, now, that I can't precisely say. In business like this, you see, it is very hard to keep exact accounts. I only know, that I paid everything back that I could scrape together. Sometimes I really didn't know what to do next. (*Smiles.*) Then I used to sit down here and imagine, that a very rich old gentleman was in love with me.

MRS. LINDEN. What! Which gentleman?

NORA. Oh! a mere story;—that he was now dead, and that when his will was opened, there stood in large letters: 'Pay over at once everything of which I die possessed to that charming person, Mrs. Nora Helmer. . .'

MRS. LINDEN. But, dear Nora, what gentleman was it?

NORA. Dear, dear, can't you understand? The old gentleman never existed: it was only what I used to sit down and think, again and again, when I positively had no notion where I could get any money from. But it doesn't matter now; the tiresome old creature may stay wherever he is, for aught I care; I don't trouble my head about him, or his will; for now I am freed from all further anxiety. (*Springing up.*) Oh, Christina, the thought of it does one good. Free from cares! Free, quite free. To be able to play and romp about with the children; to have things tasteful and refined in the house, exactly as Torvald likes it all to be! And think, we shall soon be having spring, with the glorious blue sky. Perhaps then we shall be able to have a short outing. Oh! perhaps I shall get a peep of the sea again. Oh, yes! indeed it is wonderful to live and be happy.

(*The hall-door bell rings.*)

MRS. LINDEN (*rising*). There is a ring. Perhaps I had better be going.

NORA. No; do stay. I am certain nobody will come in here. It is sure to be somebody to see Torvald.

ELLEN (*in the door to the hall*). If you please, ma'am, there is a gentleman who wishes to speak to Mr. Helmer.

Nora. The Bank Manager, you mean.

Ellen. Yes, ma'am, if you please, ma'am;—but I didn't know, as the Doctor is with him . . .

Nora. Where is the gentleman?

Krogstad (*in the doorway to the hall*). It is I, Mrs. Helmer.

(Mrs. Linden *is confused, recovers herself, and turns away to the window.*)

Nora (*goes a step towards him, excited, half aloud*). You? What does this mean? What do you want to speak with my husband about?

Krogstad. Bank business—to a certain extent. I hold a small post in the Joint Stock Bank, and your husband is now to be our chief, I hear.

Nora. So you wish to speak about . . . ?

Krogstad. Only about tiresome business, Mrs. Helmer; nothing in the world else.

Nora. Then will you be so kind as to take a seat in his office, over there? (Krogstad *goes. She bows indifferently, while she closes the door into the hall. Then she walks to the fireplace and looks at the fire.*)

Mrs. Linden. Nora, who was that man?

Nora. A Mr. Krogstad. He used to be in the law.

Mrs. Linden. So it was really he!

Nora. Do you know the man?

Mrs. Linden. I used to know him,—many years ago. He was in our town a long time, as government lawyer.

Nora. Yes; he was.

Mrs. Linden. How altered he is!

NORA. He was very unhappily married.

MRS. LINDEN. And is he now a widower?

NORA. With a whole troop of children. There! now it's burning properly. (*She shuts the stove door, and pushes the rocking-chair a little aside.*)

MRS. LINDEN. He takes up many kinds of business, people say.

NORA. Does he? I dare say. I don't know . . . But don't let us think of business; it is so tiresome.

(Doctor Rank *comes out of* Helmer's *room.*)

DOCTOR RANK (*still in the doorway*). No, no; I won't disturb you. I'll just go and chat to your wife for a little while. (*Shuts the door and sees* Mrs. Linden.) Oh, I beg your pardon. I am in the way here, too.

NORA. No, not in the least. (*Introduces them.*) Doctor Rank—Mrs. Linden.

RANK. Oh, indeed, that is a name often heard in this house. I think I just passed you on the stairs, as we entered.

MRS. LINDEN. Yes; I go so very slowly. I can't bear much going up-stairs.

RANK. Oh, I see; some slight accident.

MRS. LINDEN. It is really due to over-exertion.

RANK. No worse than that? Ah! then you have come to town, to rest yourself at all the entertainments.

MRS. LINDEN. I have come here to look for work.

RANK. May I ask if that is an approved remedy for over-exertion?

MRS. LINDEN. One must live, Doctor Rank.

RANK. Yes, the general view of the matter appears to be, that it is necessary.

NORA. Come, Doctor Rank, you yourself want to live.

RANK. To be sure I do. However miserable I am, I should like to continue to be tortured as long as possible. My patients all cherish the same wish. It is just the same with people who are morally rotten. At this very moment, Helmer has got talking to him precisely such a moral hospital-inmate as I mean.

MRS. LINDEN (*catching her breath*). Ah !

NORA. Whom do you mean ?

RANK. Oh, it's a fellow called Krogstad, a lawyer, a man you know nothing whatever about ;—rotten to the very core of his character. But even he began the conversation, as though he were going to say something very important, by saying he must live.

NORA. Indeed ? Then what did he want to talk to Torvald about ?

RANK. I really don't know that ; I only heard, that it had something to do with the Joint Stock Bank.

NORA. I didn't know that Krog—that this Mr. Krogstad had anything to do with the Bank.

RANK. He has some sort of post there. (*To* Mrs. Linden.) I don't know whether in your part of the country, too, there are to be found the sort of men who haunt the place, only to scent out moral rottenness, and thus get some advantageous post or another. The healthy may find themselves nicely left outside.

MRS. LINDEN. Well, after all, it is the sick who most need, that we should open the door and let them safely in.

RANK (*shrugging his shoulders*). Yes, that is just it.

And it is that very consideration which turns society into an hospital.

(Nora, *deep in her own thoughts, breaks into half choked laughter and claps her hands*.)

RANK. What are you laughing about? Do you know what society is?

NORA. What do I care about stupid 'society'? I was laughing over something quite different, something awfully funny. Tell me, Doctor Rank; are all the people employed at the Bank now dependent on Torvald?

RANK. Is that what strikes you as so awfully funny?

NORA (*smiles and hums*). Leave me alone, leave me alone. (*Walks about the room*.) Yes, to think that we,—that Torvald has now so much influence over so many people, really does give me enormous satisfaction. (*Takes the box from her pocket*.) Doctor Rank, will you have a maccaroon?

RANK. Oh, dear, dear! Maccaroons! I thought they were contraband here.

NORA. Yes; . . . but these are some Christina brought me.

MRS. LINDEN. What did you say, dear? I?

NORA. Oh, well, dear me! You needn't be so frightened. You couldn't possibly know, that Torvald has forbidden them. The fact is, he is afraid I might spoil my teeth. But, oh, bother, just for once! It won't hurt, will it, Doctor Rank? (*Puts a maccaroon into his mouth*.) And you too, Christina. And I will have one at the same time,—only a tiny one, or at most, two. (*Walks about again*) Yes, I really am now in a state of extraordinary happiness. There is only one thing in the world, that I should really like immensely to do.

RANK. Well, and what's that?

NORA. There's something that I should immensely like to say, so that Torvald could hear it.

RANK. And why can't you say it?

NORA. Oh! I daren't; because it sounds so ugly.

MRS. LINDEN. Ugly?

RANK. In that case, I would not advise you to say it. But you might say it to us, at any rate . . . Pluck up your courage! What is it that you would like to say, so that Helmer could hear it . . ?

NORA. I should like to shout with all my heart . . . Oh! dash it all.

RANK. Are you out of your mind?

MRS. LINDEN. My dearest Nora!

RANK. Say it. There he is.

NORA (*hides the maccaroon box*). Hush-sh-sh. (*Helmer comes out of his room, with his overcoat on his arm and his hat in his hand.*)

NORA (*going towards him*). Well, Torvald dear, and have you got rid of him?

HELMER. Yes; he's gone at last.

NORA. May I introduce you?—this is Christina, who has come to town.

HELMER. Christina? Pardon me, but I don't know . . .

NORA. Mrs. Linden, Torvald dear—Christina Linden.

HELMER. Ah, indeed! You are an early friend of my wife's, I dare say.

MRS. LINDEN. Yes; we knew each other in old times.

NORA. And now, only fancy! She has taken this long journey, in order to speak to you.

HELMER. To speak to me!

MRS. LINDEN. Well, not actually . . .

NORA. The fact is, Christina is extraordinarily clever in counting-house work, to begin with; and then she has such a great wish to work under a really able man, in order to learn even more than she knows already.

HELMER. Very sensible indeed!

NORA. And when she heard you were made Bank Manager,—the news came by telegram,—she started off and came here as fast as she could; and, Torvald dear, for my sake, you can do something for Christina. Now can't you?

HELMER. It might not be impossible. I conclude you are a widow?

MRS. LINDEN. Yes.

HELMER. And have already had some experience in office-work?

MRS. LINDEN. Yes, to some extent.

HELMER. Well, then, it is highly probable I can find a niche for you.

NORA (*clapping her hands*). There now! there now!

HELMER. You have just come at a lucky moment, Mrs. Linden.

MRS. LINDEN. Oh! how can I thank you enough?

HELMER. There is no occasion for it. (*Puts his overcoat on.*) But to-day you must excuse me.

RANK. Wait; I'll go with you. (*Fetches his fur-lined coat from the hall and warms it at the fire.*)

NORA. Don't be out long, dear Torvald.

HELMER. Only an hour; not longer.

NORA. Are you going also, Christina?

MRS. LINDEN (*putting on her walking things*). Yes; I must be off now and look for lodgings.

HELMER. Then perhaps we can go down the street together.

NORA (*helping her*). How vexatious that we should have no spare room to offer you; but it really is quite impossible.

MRS. LINDEN. What are you dreaming about? Good-bye, dear Nora, and thank you for all your kindness. .

NORA. Good-bye for a little while. Of course you'll come back this evening. And you too, Doctor Rank. What? if you feel well enough? Of course you will. Only be sure you wrap up warmly. (*They go out talking into the hall. Children's voices are heard outside on the doorsteps.*) There they are! there they are! (*She runs to the door and opens it. Mary Ann, the nurse, comes in with the children.*)

NORA. Come in! come in! (*Bends down and kisses the children.*) Oh! you sweet, blessed . . . Do you see them, Christina? Aren't they darlings?

RANK. Don't let's stand here in the draught, talking folly.

HELMER. Come, Mrs. Linden ; people who are not mothers, won't be able to stand it, if they stay here any longer. (*Doctor* Rank, Helmer, *and* Mrs. Linden *go.* Mary Ann *enters the room with the children ;* Nora *also, and she shuts the door.*)

NORA. How fresh and merry you look ! And what rosy cheeks you have !—like apples and roses. (*The children talk all at once to her, during the following.*) And so you have been having great fun ? That is splendid. Oh, really ! you have been giving Emmy and Bob a ride on your sledge. What ! both at once ? Dear me ! you are quite a man, Ivar. Oh, give her to me a little, Mary Ann. My sweet little dolly Baby! (*Takes the smallest from the nurse, and dances it up and down.*) Yes, yes, mother will dance with Bob, too. What! did you have a game of snow-balls, as well ? Oh ! I ought to have been there. No, leave them, Mary Ann ; I will take their things off myself. No, no, let me do it ; it is so amusing. Go to the nursery for a while ; you look so frozen. There is some hot coffee for you, on the stove. (*The nurse goes to the room on the left.* Nora *takes off the children's things, and throws them down anyhow ; while she lets the children talk to each other and to her.*) Really ! Then there was a big dog, who ran after you ? But I'm sure he didn't bite you ? No ; dogs don't bite dear dolly little children. Don't peep into those parcels, Ivar. You want to know what that is ? Yes, you are the only people who shall know. Oh, no, no, that is not behaving prettily. What ! must we have a game ? What shall it be, then ? Hide and seek ?

Yes, let us play hide and seek. Bob shall hide first. Am I to? Very well; I will hide first.

(*She and the children play, with laughing and shouting in the room and the adjacent one to the right. At last,* Nora *hides under the table; the children come rushing in to look for her, but cannot find her; hear her half-choked laughter; rush to the table; lift up the cover, and see her. Shouts of joy. She creeps out, as though to frighten them. Fresh shouts. Meanwhile there has been a knock at the hall door. No one has noticed it. Now the door is half opened, and* Krogstad *is seen. He waits a little; the game is continued.*)

KROGSTAD. Excuse me, Mrs. Helmer—

NORA (*with a suppressed cry, turns round and half jumps up*). Oh! what do you want?

KROGSTAD. Excuse me; the inner hall door was ajar;—somebody must have forgotten to shut it.

NORA (*standing up*). My husband is not at home, Mr. Krogstad.

KROGSTAD. I know it.

NORA. Indeed! Then what do you want here?

KROGSTAD. To say a few words to you.

NORA. To me? (*To the children softly.*) Go in to the nursery to Mary Ann. What, dear? No, the strange man won't hurt Mamma. When he is gone, we will go on playing. (*She leads the children into the left-hand room and shuts the door behind them.*)

NORA (*uneasy, in anxiety*). It was with me you wished to speak?

KROGSTAD. Yes.

NORA. To-day? But it is not the first day of the month yet . . .

KROGSTAD. No; to-day is Christmas Eve. It will depend upon yourself how far you enjoy your Christmas.

NORA. What do you really want of me? I certainly can't to-day—

KROGSTAD. We won't discuss that just at present. It is about another matter. You have a minute to spare?

NORA. Oh, yes, certainly; I have that, although—

KROGSTAD. Good. I was sitting over there in the Restaurant, and I saw your husband cross the street.

NORA. Yes; well?

KROGSTAD. With a lady.

NORA. And what then?

KROGSTAD. May I ask if the lady was a certain Mrs. Linden?

NORA. Yes.

KROGSTAD. Who has just arrived?

NORA. Yes. This morning.

KROGSTAD. I suppose she is an intimate friend of yours?

NORA. Certainly she is. But I don't understand . . .

KROGSTAD. I used to know her, too.

NORA. I know you did.

KROGSTAD. Really? Then you know all about it. I thought as much. Now, may I ask plainly and bluntly, whether Mrs. Linden is to have some post in the Bank?

NORA. How can you allow yourself to catechize me in this way—you, a subordinate official of my husband's? But since you have asked, you shall know Yes, Mrs. Linden is to be employed at the Bank. And it is I who spoke for her, Mr. Krogstad. Now you know.

KROGSTAD. Then my inference was right.

NORA (*walking up and down*). Oh! I should imagine one always has a little wee bit of influence. It doesn't follow, that because one is only a woman, that . . . When one is in a dependent position, Mr. Krogstad, one ought to take the greatest care not to offend anybody who—hm—

KROGSTAD. Who has influence?

NORA. Yes; just so.

KROGSTAD (*taking another tone*). Mrs. Helmer, will you have the kindness to employ your influence in my favour?

NORA. What? How do you mean?

KROGSTAD. Will you be so obliging as to take care, that I retain my dependent position at the Bank?

NORA. What is all this about? Who wants to take your post away?

KROGSTAD. Oh, you needn't pretend ignorance towards me. I can very well comprehend, that it cannot be pleasant for your friend to expose herself to constant collision with me; and I can also comprehend now, whom I have to thank for my dismissal.

NORA. But I assure you . . .

KROGSTAD. Oh, yes ; make no bones about it : there

is yet time; and I advise you to use your influence to prevent it.

NORA. But, Mr. Krogstad, I have absolutely no influence.

KROGSTAD. None? It seems to me you were saying just now yourself—

NORA. Of course you were not to understand me in that sense. I! How can you think I should have such influence as that over my husband?

KROGSTAD. Oh, I've known your husband since our College days. I don't think he is firmer than other husbands are.

NORA. If you talk disparagingly of my husband, I must request you to go.

KROGSTAD. You are very courageous, my dear madam.

NORA. I am no longer afraid of you. When New Year's Day is over, I shall soon be out of the whole difficulty.

KROGSTAD (*controlling himself more*). Now just listen to me, Mrs. Helmer. If needs be, I shall fight as though it were for my life, in order to keep my small post in the Bank.

NORA. Yes; it really looks as if you would.

KROGSTAD. It is not only on account of the pay; that is the part of it which matters to me least. But it is something else. Well, I suppose I'd better make a clean breast of it. Look here; it's this. Of course you know just what everybody else knows,—that many years ago, I once got into trouble.

NORA. I think I heard something of the sort.

KROGSTAD. The matter never came into Court; but from that moment, all paths were, as it were, barricaded to me. Then I threw myself into the kind of business which you know about. I was obliged to snatch at something; and I may say this much: I wasn't the worst of the men in that line. But now I ought to clear out of all business of that sort. My sons are growing up; on their account, I must try to win back as much respectability as I possibly can. In that direction, this post at the Bank was the first step of the stairway. And now your husband wants to kick me off the step and back into the mire.

NORA. But I do assure you, Mr. Krogstad, it is really not in my power to help you.

KROGSTAD. That is because you will not; but I have the means of compelling you to help me.

NORA. You don't intend to tell my husband, that I owe you money?

KROGSTAD. Hm. Suppose I were to tell him?

NORA. It would be scandalous of you. (*Choking with suppressed tears.*) This secret, which is my joy and my pride, that he should learn it in such a vulgar, blunt way;—from you! You want to put me to the most terrible annoyance.

KROGSTAD. Only annoyance?

NORA (*hotly*). But just do it; the consequences will be worse for you than anybody else; for then my husband will see clearly what a bad man you are, and then you certainly will not keep your post.

KROGSTAD. I asked if it were only domestic unpleasantness that you were afraid of?

NORA. If my husband gets to know about it, he will of course pay the rest without delay; and then we shall have nothing more to do with you.

KROGSTAD (*stepping a pace nearer*). Listen, Mrs. Helmer: either you have rather a weak memory, or you don't know much about business. I must get you to go more deeply into the matter.

NORA. How will you do that?

KROGSTAD. When your husband was ill, you came to me to borrow £300 of me.

NORA. I knew nobody else.

KROGSTAD. I promised to find you the money.

NORA. And you did find it.

KROGSTAD. I promised to find you the money, under certain conditions. You were just then so excited about your husband's illness, and so anxious to get hold of the money for your journey, that I think you took no heed of all the attendant circumstances. It is therefore, not out of order for me to remind you of them. Now, I promised to find you the money, in exchange for an acknowledgment, which I drew up.

NORA. Yes, and I signed it.

KROGSTAD. Very well. But then I added a few lines, whereby your father became security for the debt. Your father was to sign this.

NORA. Was to? He did sign.

KROGSTAD. I had left the date blank: that is to say, your father was to insert the date on which he signed the document. Do you recollect this, Mrs. Helmer?

NORA. Yes, I believe . . .

KROGSTAD. Thereupon I gave you the acknowledgment, that you might send it to your father. Was not that so?

NORA. Yes.

KROGSTAD. And of course you did so without delay; for within five or six days, you brought me back the acknowledgment duly signed by your father. Then you received from me the sum promised.

NORA. Well, to be sure; have I not paid it back punctually?

KROGSTAD. Very fairly; yes. But let us return to the matter we were speaking of. You were in great trouble at the time, Mrs. Helmer.

NORA. I was indeed.

KROGSTAD. Your father, too, was very seriously ill, I believe.

NORA. He was on his death-bed.

KROGSTAD. And died soon after?

NORA. Yes.

KROGSTAD. Now, just tell me, Mrs. Helmer, whether by any chance you happen to recollect which day he died,—which day of the month, I mean.

NORA. Father died on the twenty-ninth of September.

KROGSTAD. Quite correct; I have made inquiries about it. And therefore there is a peculiarity which I cannot explain. (*Takes a paper from his pocket.*)

NORA. What peculiarity? I do not know . . .

KROGSTAD. The peculiarity, dear Mrs. Helmer, is, that your father signed this acknowledgment three days after his death.

NORA. What? I don't understand.

KROGSTAD. Your father died on the twenty-ninth of September. But just look here. Here your father has dated his signature 'October the 2nd.' Is not that peculiar, Mrs. Helmer? (Nora *is silent.*) Can you explain that to me? (Nora *continues silent.*) It is also striking, that the words 'October the 2nd' and the year are not in your father's handwriting, but in one which I believe I know. Now this may be explained by supposing, that your father forgot to date it, and that somebody added the date by guess work, before the fact of his death was known. There is nothing improper in that proceeding. But it is the signature of his name that my question relates to. And is it genuine, Mrs. Helmer? Was it really your father, who with his own hand, set his name here?

NORA (*after a short silence throws her head back and looks defiantly at him*). No, it is not; it is I, who wrote papa's name there.

KROGSTAD. And are you aware, moreover, that that is a dangerous admission?

NORA. Why? You will soon get your money.

KROGSTAD. May I be permitted one more question: Why did you not send the document to your father?

NORA. It was impossible. Father was then dangerously ill. If I had asked him for his signature, I should also have had to tell him what I wanted the money for. But in his condition, I really could not tell him, that my husband's life hung by a thread. It was quite impossible.

KROGSTAD. Then it would have been better for you to give up the journey abroad.

NORA. That was impossible, too.   My husband's
life depended on that journey. I could not give it up.

KROGSTAD. But did you not consider, then, that it
was a fraud on me?

NORA. I could not take any heed of that. I did
not care in the least about you. I could not endure
you, on account of all the hard-hearted difficulties you
made, although you knew what danger my husband
was in.

KROGSTAD. Mrs. Helmer, you have evidently no
clear idea what you have been really guilty of. But I
can assure you it was nothing different from this, nor
worse than this, that I once did, and that destroyed
my entire position in society.

NORA. You? Do you want to make me believe,
that you ever undertook to do anything courageous, in
order to save your wife's life?

KROGSTAD. The laws do not inquire into motives.

NORA. Then we must have very bad laws.

KROGSTAD. Bad, or not bad,—if I lay this document before a court of law, you will be judged according to the laws.

NORA. That I do not in the least believe. Do you
mean to tell me, that a daughter has not the right to
spare her old father, on his death-bed, care and worry?
Do you mean to say, that a wife has not the right to
save her husband's life? I don't know the law precisely, but I am convinced, that somewhere or another,
the law must contain leave for me to have done such
things.   And you don't know it?—you, a lawyer!
You must be a bad lawyer, Mr. Krogstad.

KROGSTAD. I dare say. But business—such business as ours here—you believe that I do understand? Very well. Now, do as you please. But this I do say to you : that if I am turned out of society a second time, you shall keep me company. (*He bows and goes out through the hall.*)

NORA (*stands awhile thinking ; then she throws her head back*). Never! To try to frighten me! I am not so simple as that. (*Begins folding the children's clothes ; soon pauses.*) But . . . no ; but that is quite impossible. I did it from love.

THE CHILDREN (*in the left door*). Mamma, the strange man is gone now.

NORA. Yes, yes ; I know. But don't tell any one about the strange man. Do you hear? Not even papa.

THE CHILDREN. No, mamma ; but now will you play with us again ?

NORA. No, no ; not now.

THE CHILDREN. Oh, do, mamma. You did promise.

NORA. Yes ; but I can't just now. Run to the nursery ; I have so much to do. Run along, run along. my dear, good children. (*Cautiously she compels them to go into the inner room, and shuts the door behind them.*)

NORA (*throws herself on the sofa, takes a piece of embroidery and does a few stitches, but soon pauses*). No. (*Throws the embroidery down, stands up, goes to the door towards the hall, and calls out*) Ellen, bring in the Christmas tree. (*Goes to the left-hand table and opens the drawer; stands again, thoughtful.*) No; but that is quite impossible.

ELLEN (*with the Christmas-tree*). Where shall I place it, if you please, ma'am?

NORA. There, in the middle of the room.

ELLEN. Shall I bring in anything else?

NORA. No, thank you; I have what I want.

(Ellen, *who has put down the tree, goes out again.*)

NORA (*busy dressing the tree*). There must be a candle here, and some flowers there.—The horrid man!—Nonsense, nonsense; there is nothing wrong in it . . . The Christmas-tree shall be beautiful. I will do everything that gives you pleasure, Torvald; I will sing, and dance, and . . .

(Helmer *enters from out of doors, with a bundle of documents under his arm.*)

NORA. Oh! are you back already?

HELMER. Yes. Has anybody been here?

NORA. Here? No.

HELMER. Curious! I saw Krogstad come out of the house.

NORA. Did you? Oh, yes, it is true he was here for a minute.

HELMER. Nora, I can see from your manner he has been here, and asked you to put in a good word for him.

NORA. Yes.

HELMER. And you were to do it as of your own accord? You were to say nothing to me of his having been here. Did he not ask that it should be so?

NORA. Yes, Torvald; but . . .

HELMER. Nora, Nora! and you could be induced to do that? to allow yourself to be drawn into talk with such a man, and give him a promise about it. And then tell me an untruth about it into the bargain!

NORA. An untruth?

HELMER. Didn't you say nobody had been here? (*Threatens with his finger.*) My lark must never do that again. A singing-bird must have a clean little beak to sing with; and never sing false notes. (*Puts his arm round her.*) That's true, isn't it? Yes, I knew it. (*Lets her go.*) And now we'll say no more about it. (*Sits down before the fire.*) Oh, how comfortable and quiet it is here. (*Glances into his documents.*)

NORA (*busy with the tree, after a short silence*). Torvald.

HELMER. Yes.

NORA. I am so excessively delighted over the Stenborgs' costume ball, the day after to-morrow.

HELMER. And I am so excessively curious to see what you will surprise me with.

NORA. Oh! that's the tiresome part of it.

HELMER. How do you mean?

NORA. I can't find anything to suit me. Everything seems so silly and meaningless.

HELMER. Has my little Nora arrived at *that* opinion?

NORA (*behind his chair, with her arms on the back*). Are you very busy, Torvald?

HELMER. Eh?

NORA. What sort of papers are those?

HELMER. Papers concerning the Bank.

NORA. Already?

HELMER. I got the retiring authorities to give me full power beforehand, to make the necessary changes in the staff and method of working. This is what I must spend my Christmas week in arranging. By New Year's Day, I will have everything in order.

NORA. Then this is why that poor Krogstad . . .

HELMER. H—m . . .

NORA (*continues leaning over the chair, strokes his hair slowly*). If your work were not so pressing, I should ask you a great, great favour, Torvald.

HELMER. Let's hear it. What can it be?

NORA. Nobody has such refined taste as you have. Now I should so love to look well at the costume ball. Torvald, dear, couldn't you take me in hand and settle what character I am to appear in, and how my costume ought to be arranged?

HELMER. Is that obstinate little head of yours tired out at last, and looking about for somebody to save it from destruction?

NORA. Yes, Torvald. Without you, I am utterly helpless.

HELMER. Well, well; I'll think it over; we shall be sure to hit upon something together.

NORA. Oh, how kind and good that is of you! (*Goes to the tree again; pause.*) How pretty the red flowers look! But, by the bye, was the thing which Krogstad got into trouble about, years ago, really so bad?

HELMER. Forged a name, that's all. Have you any notion what that means?

NORA. Mustn't he have done it from need?

HELMER. Yes, or as so many others do it, from

heedlessness. I am not so heartless as to judge anybody absolutely, from such a transaction alone.

NORA. No; that's just what I thought you would say, Torvald.

HELMER. Many a man can lift himself up again morally, if he openly recognizes his offence, and undergoes its punishment.

NORA. Punishment?

HELMER. But Krogstad didn't set about it in that way: he tried to work his way out of it by dodges and tricks; and by that very means, he has morally ruined himself.

NORA. Do you think that it . . . ?

HELMER. Only just think how a man, so conscious of guilt as that, must go about everywhere lying, and a hypocrite, and an actor; how he must wear a mask towards his neighbour, and even his wife and children. Its affecting the children is the worst part of it, Nora.

NORA. Why?

HELMER. Because such a misty atmosphere of lying brings contagion into the whole family. Every breath the children draw contains some germ of evil.

NORA (*closer behind him*). Are you quite sure?

HELMER. As a lawyer, darling child, I have remarked that, many a time. Nearly all men who go to ruin early, have had untruthful mothers.

NORA. Why should it be—mothers?

HELMER. In most cases, it comes from the mother; but the father naturally works in the same direction. Every lawyer has reason to know that. And Krogstad has actually been poisoning his own children for years past, by lying and acting a part; that is precisely why I call him morally lost. (*Stretches out his hands to her.*) This is the reason why my dear little Nora must promise me not to plead on his behalf. Shake hands upon it. Come, come; what's that? Give me your hand. That's right. Then it's a bargain. I do assure you it would have been impossible to me to work with him. I literally feel bodily discomfort when I am in any proximity to such people.

NORA (*takes her hand away and walks to the other side of the Christmas-tree*). How warm it is here! And I have so much to do, still.

HELMER (*rises and puts his papers together*). Yes, I must take care to get some of these papers read through before dinner; and I will think over your costume, too. And I should not be surprised, if I were to get some trifle ready, which might be hung in gilt paper on the Christmas-tree. (*Lays his hand upon her head.*) My dear little lark! (*He goes into his room and shuts the door behind him.*)

NORA (*slowly, after a pause*). What was it? It can't be so . . . That is impossible. It must be impossible.

MARY ANN (*in the left door*). The little ones are begging so prettily to come in to mamma.

NORA. No, no; don't let them come in to me. Let them stay with you, Mary Ann.

MARY ANN. Very well, ma'am. (*Shuts the door.*)

NORA (*pale with terror*). I ruin my children . . . poison my home. (*Short pause. She raises her head proudly.*) That is not true. It is never, and can never be, true.

ACT II.

THE SAME ROOM.

*In the corner beside the piano, stands the Christmas-
tree, stripped, shabby, and with the candles burnt out.
On the sofa, Nora's walking things.)*

(Nora, *alone, is in the room; she walks about restlessly;
at last she stands by the sofa and takes up her
cloak.*)

NORA (*takes off her cloak again*). There was somebody coming. (*Goes to the door; listens.*) No; nobody.
Nobody is likely to come to-day, Christmas Day, nor
to-morrow either. But perhaps .. (*Opens the door and
peeps out.*) No. Nothing in the letter-box; it's quite
empty. (*Comes to the front of the stage.*) Stuff and
nonsense! Of course he will do nothing serious in it.
Nothing of the kind can possibly happen. It is impossible. Why, I have three little children.

(Mary Ann *comes out of the left room, with a large
card-board box.*)

MARY ANN. At last I've found the box, with the
masquerade dress.

NORA. Thanks; put it down on the table there.

MARY ANN (*does so*). But it is still very much out
of order, ma'am.

Nora. Oh, I wish I could tear it into a hundred thousand pieces.

Mary Ann. Good gracious me, ma'am! Why, it can be easily put to rights; it only wants a little patience.

Nora. Yes; I will go to Mrs. Linden, and get her to help me.

Mary Ann. What! out again, ma'am? In this dreadful weather? You'll catch your death of cold, ma'am, and be quite ill.

Nora. Oh, that's not the worst thing which could happen. What are the children doing?

Mary Ann. They're playing with their Christmas presents, dear little things; but . . .

Nora. Do they often ask after me?

Mary Ann. Well, you see, ma'am, they have been so used to having their mamma always with them.

Nora. Yes; but, Mary Ann, henceforth I can't have them so much with me.

Mary Ann. Well, ma'am, little children get used to anything.

Nora. Do you think they do? Do you believe, that they would forget their mamma, if she went quite away?

Mary Ann. Gracious me, ma'am; quite away!

Nora. Tell me, Mary Ann,—I've so often wondered about it,—how could you bring yourself to place your child out among strangers?

Mary Ann. But I was obliged to, if I wanted to come as nurse to my little Miss Nora, ma'am.

Nora. Yes; but that you could be willing to do it·

MARY ANN. When I could get such a good place, ma'am? A poor girl who's been in trouble, could only be very glad to come. For that wicked man did nothing for me.

NORA. But of course your daughter has forgotten you?

MARY ANN. Oh! no, ma'am, not in the least. She wrote to me, both when she was confirmed, and when she got married.

NORA (*embracing her*). Dear Mary Ann, you were a good mother to me, when I was a little girl.

MARY ANN. My poor little Miss Nora had no mother but me.

NORA. And if my little children had nobody else, I am sure you would . . . Nonsense, nonsense. (*Opens the box.*) Go to them in the nursery. Now I must . . . To-morrow you shall see how beautifully this dress suits me.

MARY ANN. Yes, ma'am, I'm sure there will be nobody at the whole ball so beautiful as my Miss Nora. (*She goes into the left room.*)

NORA (*begins taking the costume out of the box ; but soon pushes it all away from her*). Oh, if I dared go out! If only nobody would come! If only nothing would happen, here, at home, meanwhile! Rubbish! nobody will come. Only not to think . . . Stroke one's muff smooth! Beautiful gloves, beautiful gloves . . . Away with the whole thing, away with it . . . One, two, three, four, five, six. (*With a cry.*) Oh! there they come . . . (*Would go towards the door, but stands undecided.*)

E

(Mrs. Linden *comes from the hall, where she has taken off her things.*)

NORA. Oh, it is you, Christina. Is nobody else there? How delightful of you to come !

MRS. LINDEN. I hear you have called at my lodgings to ask for me.

NORA. Yes, I was just passing. There is something I wanted you to help me with. Let us sit here on the sofa. Look here. To-morrow evening, there is a costume ball at Consul Stenborg's overhead ; and now Torvald wants me to appear as a Neapolitan fisher-girl, and dance the Tarantella, because I learnt it in Capri.

MRS. LINDEN. I see, dear. Then you are to give quite a representation of the character?

NORA. Yes ; Torvald wishes it. Look ! here is the costume. Torvald had it made for me in Italy ; but now it is all so torn, and I hardly know . . .

MRS. LINDEN. Oh ! we'll soon set that to rights for you. It is only the trimming which has got loose, here and there. Have you a needle and thread? Ah ! there's the very thing we want.

NORA. How kind it is of you !

MRS. LINDEN (*sewing*). Then you're going to dress up to-morrow, Nora, are you? I tell you what,—I shall come in for a moment, in order to see you in all your glory. But I have quite forgotten to thank you for the pleasant evening you gave me yesterday.

NORA (*gets up and walks across the room*). Ah ! yesterday it didn't seem to me so pleasant here as it generally is . . . You should have come to town a

little sooner, Christina. Yes, Torvald certainly knows
how to make our home beautiful and pleasant.

Mrs. Linden. And so do you, I think; or you
would not be your father's daughter. But tell me,—
is Doctor Rank always so depressed as he was yesterday evening?

Nora. It was painfully striking yesterday. But he
really has symptoms of a very dangerous illness which
accounts for it. He has spinal consumption, poor
wretch. You see, his father was an awful man, who
did all sorts of wrong things, and so of course his son
has been ill from his childhood.

Mrs. Linden (*lets her sewing fall into her lap*). But,
my dearest, loveliest Nora, how do you learn such
things?

Nora (*walking*). Oh! when one has three children,
one is sometimes called upon by . . . by women, who
have a little medical knowledge; and they will chat
about one thing and another.

Mrs. Linden (*goes on sewing; short pause*). Does
Doctor Rank come here every day?

Nora. He never misses. He has been Torvald's
friend from boyhood, you know, and is a good
friend of mine, too. Doctor Rank is quite one of the
family.

Mrs. Linden. But just tell me, dear; is the man
quite honest? I mean, doesn't he like saying flatter-
ing things to people?

Nora. On the contrary. What makes you think
so?

Mrs. Linden. When you introduced us yesterday,

he declared he had often heard my name in the house;
but then I noticed your husband had scarcely any idea
who I was. How, then, could Doctor Rank?

NORA. You are right, Christina. But you see,
Torvald loves me so indescribably much ; and that is
why he wants to have me all to himself, as he expresses it. When we first married, he was almost
jealous, if I did but mention one of the people I loved
at home ; so naturally I left it off. But I often talk
to Doctor Rank about it, for he loves to hear me, you
know.

MRS. LINDEN. Now, listen, Nora ; you are still just
like a child in many things. I am somewhat older
than you are, and have a little more experience. I
will tell you something : you ought to put an end to
the whole affair with this Doctor.

NORA. What affair ought I to put an end to?

MRS. LINDEN. Both affairs, it seems to me. Yesterday you were telling me about a rich admirer, who
was to furnish you with money.

NORA. Yes, and who doesn't exist, more's the pity.
But what then ?

MRS. LINDEN. Has Doctor Rank property ?

NORA. Yes, he has.

MRS. LINDEN. And nobody to provide for ?

NORA. No ; nobody. But—

MRS. LINDEN. And he comes here every day ?

NORA. Yes ; I tell you he never misses.

MRS. LINDEN. But how can he, as a gentleman, be
so needy ?

NORA. I really don't understand you.

MRS. LINDEN. Don't pretend, Nora. Don't you suppose I guess from whom you borrowed the £300?

NORA. Are you out of your senses? Can you think anything of the sort? A friend of the family, who comes here every day to us! What a frightfully torturing state of things it would be!

MRS. LINDEN. Then it really is not he?

NORA. No; that I do assure you. It never for a moment occurred to me to ask him. Besides, at that time, he had nothing to lend; it was later that he came into his property.

MRS. LINDEN. Well, that was certainly lucky for you, Nora dear.

NORA. No, really, it never would have struck me to ask Doctor Rank. However, I am certain, that in case I did ask him—

MRS. LINDEN. But of course you never would?

NORA. I should think not, indeed. I do not believe I can imagine its being necessary. But I am firmly convinced, that if I spoke to Doctor Rank—

MRS. LINDEN. Behind your husband's back?

NORA. I must get out of the other loan; that I had to manage behind his back, too. I must get out of that.

MRS. LINDEN. Yes, yes, I was saying so too, yesterday; but—

NORA (*walking up and down*). A man can get such a thing into order much better than a woman can . . .

MRS. LINDEN. Her own husband; yes.

NORA. Nonsense. (*Stands still.*) When one pays

everything off that one owes, one gets back the acknowledgment of the debt?

MRS. LINDEN. Yes, of course.

NORA. And can tear it into a hundred thousand pieces, and burn the nasty, horrid thing!

MRS. LINDEN (*looks at her fixedly, lays down her work, and gets up slowly*). Nora, you are hiding something from me.

NORA. Can you see that in my manner?

MRS. LINDEN. Since yesterday morning, something has been happening to you. Nora, what is it?

NORA (*going towards her*). Christina. (*Listens.*) Hush. There's Torvald coming home. Here, go and sit with the children, while you are doing that work. Torvald can't bear to see dressmaking. Let Mary Ann help you.

MRS. LINDEN (*gathers some of the things together*). Very well; but I shan't go away, until we have spoken openly to each other.

(*She goes away to the left, as* Helmer *enters from the hall.*)

NORA (*goes to meet him*). Oh! how I have been longing to see you, Torvald dear.

HELMER. Was the dressmaker here?

NORA. No; Christina. She is helping me to get my costume into order. You will see I shall look perfectly charming.

HELMER. Yes; wasn't that an extremely lucky thought of mine?

NORA. Glorious! But is it not also very nice of me to give in to you?

HELMER (*takes her under the chin*). Nice of you,—that you give in to your own husband! Why, you little rogue, I know very well you didn't mean anything of the sort. But I won't disturb you. I dare say you want to be fitting on your dress.

NORA. And I dare say you're going to work?

HELMER. Yes (*shows her a bundle of documents*). Look here. I have been down at the Bank. (*Is about to go to his room.*)

NORA. Torvald.

HELMER (*stands still*). Yes.

NORA. If your little squirrel were to ask you for something really very prettily . . .

HELMER. Then?

NORA. Would you do it?

HELMER. Naturally I should first expect to be told what it is.

NORA. The little squirrel would jump about and perform all sorts of funny tricks, if you would be amiable, and do as you are asked.

HELMER. Come, then; out with it!

NORA. The little lark would twitter round in all the rooms, loud and soft by turns . . .

HELMER. Oh, there's nothing in that. She does all that, as it is.

NORA. I would act a fairy, and dance in the moonlight, Torvald.

HELMER. Nora, you can't mean what you were begging me about this morning?

NORA (*coming nearer*). Yes, Torvald, I do beg and pray you.

HELMER. Have you really the courage to mention the matter again to me?

NORA. Yes, yes. You must do what I want. You must let Krogstad keep his place at the Bank.

HELMER. My dear Nora, I have arranged for his place to be given to Mrs. Linden.

NORA. Yes, and that was very nice of you. But instead of Krogstad, you could dismiss some other clerk.

HELMER. This is incredible obstinacy. Because you heedlessly promised to put in a word for him, I am to . . .

NORA. Not for that reason, Torvald. It is for your own sake. The man is on the staff of some of our most scurrilous newspapers; I have heard you say so myself. He can do you such infinite harm. I am so terribly afraid of him.

HELMER. Oh, I understand; it is old recollections which are frightening you.

NORA. Why do you say that?

HELMER. Of course you are thinking of your father.

NORA. Yes, to be sure. Only call to mind what wicked men used to write about father in the papers, and how shamefully they calumniated him! I believe they really would have got him dismissed, if Government had not sent you down to look into the matter, and if you had not been so kindly and considerate towards him.

HELMER. My dear Nora, between your father and me, there is all the difference in the world. Your father was not, as an official, quite unimpeachable.

But I am; and I hope to remain so, as long as I am at my post.

NORA. Oh, no one knows what wicked men can find to say. We could be so well off now, and live so quietly and happily in our peaceful home, free from any kind of care,—you, and I, and the children, Torvald! This is why I beg you so earnestly.

HELMER. And it is just by interceding for him, that you make it impossible for me to keep him. It is already known at the Bank, that I intend to dismiss Krogstad. If it were now to be known, that the new Bank Manager let himself be talked round by his wife—

NORA. Well, what then?

HELMER. If only the obstinate little woman can get her own way, of course that is all she wants . . . I am to make myself the laughing-stock of all the clerks, and set people saying I am under all sorts of outside influence. Take my word for it, I should soon trace the consequences. And besides, there is one circumstance which makes Krogstad an impossible person to have at the Bank, while I am manager there.

NORA. What circumstance?

HELMER. In case of necessity, I could perhaps have overlooked his moral fault . . .

NORA. Yes, couldn't you, Torvald?

HELMER. And by what I hear, he must be quite competent. But we knew each other in early youth. It is one of those hasty acquaintances, which so often hamper one in later life. Well, I may just as well tell you the whole thing plainly: He calls me 'Torvald.'

And the tactless creature makes no secret of it, when other people are present. On the contrary, he fancies it justifies his taking a familiar tone with me; and so he blurts out, at every turn, 'I say, Torvald:' I do assure you it causes me most painful emotion. He would make my position at the Bank perfectly unendurable to me.

NORA. Torvald, you are not serious in saying all this.

HELMER. Not? Why not?

NORA. All these are such petty considerations.

HELMER. What are you saying? Petty— Do you consider me petty?

NORA. No, on the contrary, Torvald dear; and that is just why—

HELMER. It's all the same. You call my reasons petty; then I must be so, too. Petty! Very well, then. Now we'll put an end to this, once and for all. (*Goes to the door into the hall, and calls.*) Ellen!

NORA. What do you want?

HELMER (*searching among his papers*). To settle the thing.

(Ellen *enters.*)

HELMER. There; take that letter. Go down with it at once. Get hold of a messenger. But be quick. The address is on it. Here is the money for him.

ELLEN. Yes, sir. (*She goes with the letter.*)

HELMER (*putting his papers in order*). There! my obstinate little wife.

NORA (*breathlessly*). Torvald, what letter was that?

HELMER. Krogstad's dismissal.

NORA. Fetch it back again, Torvald. There is still
time. Oh, Torvald, get it back again. Do it for my
sake,—for your own sake,—for our children's sake.
Do you hear? Torvald, do it. You don't know
what that letter has the power to bring upon us all.

HELMER. Too late.

NORA. Yes, too late.

HELMER. Dear Nora, I forgive you for putting yourself into this state of anxiety, although it is founded
upon what is wounding to me. Yes, that is what it
really is. Or perhaps it is no offence to me, for you
to believe I should be afraid of the revenge of a dis-
graced newspaper scribbler? But I forgive it you,
because it is all the time a charming proof of your
great love for me. (*Takes her in his arms.*) We will
look at it so, my own darling Nora. Let what will
befall us, if I am called upon for it, I have not only
courage, but the strength too, you know. You shall
see that I am the man to take everything upon my
shoulders.

NORA (*suddenly terrified*). What do you mean by
that?

HELMER. Everything, I say.

NORA (*decidedly*). That you shall never, never do.

HELMER. Very well; then we will share it, Nora,
as man and wife. That's the way it shall be. (*Strokes
her.*) Are you satisfied now? Come, come, come;
don't let me see those eyes looking like a scared
dove's. The whole thing is nothing but the most
baseless fancy. Now you must act the Tarantella, and
practise the tambourine. I shall go and sit in my

inner office and shut the door between them, so that I shall hear nothing. You can make as much noise as ever you please; (*turns round in the door-way*) and when Rank comes, just tell him where I am to be found. (*He nods to her, goes into his room with his papers, and shuts the door after him.*)

NORA (*bewildered with anxiety, stands as though rooted to the ground, and whispers*). He had it in his power to do it. Yes; he did it. He did it in spite of all and everything I said. No; never that, to all Eternity. Rather anything than that! Save me! Oh, for some way out of it! (*The hall-door bell rings.*) Doctor Rank! Rather anything than that, whatever it may be. (*She recovers herself, strokes her face, goes to the door leading to the hall, and opens it. Doctor Rank is standing outside and hanging up his great coat. During the following scene, it grows dark.*) Good afternoon, Doctor Rank. I knew you by your ring. But you must not go to Torvald now; for I believe he has some work to do.

RANK. And you?

NORA (*as he walks into the room, and she shuts the door behind him*). Oh, you know perfectly well, I have always a spare moment for you.

RANK. Thank you. I shall avail myself of your kindness as long as ever I can.

NORA. What does that mean? As long as ever you can?

RANK. Yes; does that frighten you?

NORA. Well, it was such a curious expression. Is anything going to happen?

RANK. That will happen, for which I have long been prepared; but I certainly did not think it would come off so soon.

NORA (*seizing his arm*). What is it you have got to know? Doctor Rank, you must tell me.

RANK (*sitting down by the stove*). I am running downhill. There is no help for it.

NORA (*breathing with relief*). You are the one, then, who . . . ?

RANK. Who else should it be? There can be no use in deceiving one's self? I am the most miserable of all my patients, Mrs. Helmer. In the last few days, I have had a general stock-taking of my inner man. Bankruptcy! Before a month is over, I shall perhaps be food for worms in the churchyard.

NORA. Oh, what ugly things you say!

RANK. The thing itself is so cursed ugly. But the worst of it is, that so many ugly things have to be gone through first. There is only one investigation to be made, and when I have made it, I shall know pretty well at what time dissolution will begin. There is something I want to say to you about that. Helmer has stamped on his refined nature such a hatred for all that is disagreeable; I will not have him in my sick room.

NORA. Oh! but, Doctor Rank—

RANK. I will not have him in my sick room,— upon any consideration whatsoever. I close my door against him. As soon as I obtain completely certain information as to the worst, I shall send you my visiting card with a black cross on it; and then you will know, that the horrors of dissolution have begun.

NORA. Come! The way you are talking to-day is perfectly absurd. And I was so particularly anxious you should be in a really good temper.

RANK. With Death staring me in the face? And all by way of penance for the faults of another! What justice is there in that? Just such compensation is being exacted, inexorably, after one fashion or another, in every family.

NORA (*stopping her ears*). Nonsense. Do be funny, funny!

RANK. Yes, really, the whole story is only worth laughing at. My poor innocent spine must waste away, for my father's notions of amusement when he was a lieutenant in the army.

NORA (*at the left table*). I suppose he was devoted to asparagus and Strasburg pies, wasn't he?

RANK. Certainly, and to truffles.

NORA. Yes, devoted to truffles, to be sure; and to oysters, I believe.

RANK. Yes, to oysters; no need to mention that; oysters, of course.

NORA. And then all the port wine and champagne. It is sad that all these dainties should affect the bones so disastrously.

RANK. Especially when the bones so disastrously affected never got the least advantage from the dainties.

NORA. Yes; that is the saddest part of all.

RANK (*looks at her searchingly*). H—m . . .

NORA (*a moment later*). Why were you smiling?

RANK. No; it was you who smiled.

NORA. No, you, Doctor Rank.

RANK (*standing up*). You are really a greater rogue than I thought.

NORA. To-day I am just inclined to play all sorts of tricks.

RANK. It seems like it.

NORA (*with her hands on his shoulders*). Dear, good Doctor Rank, Death shall not take you away from Torvald and me.

RANK. Oh, that is a loss, I am sorry to say, you will easily get over. People who go away, are soon forgotten.

NORA (*looking at him anxiously*). Do you think so?

RANK. People make fresh ties, and then—

NORA. Who is making fresh ties?

RANK. Both you and Helmer will do it, as soon as I am gone. In fact, *you* are setting about it already, it seems to me. What was that Mrs. Linden doing here yesterday?

NORA. Oh, that's it? But you don't mean to say you're jealous of poor Christina?

RANK. Yes, I am. She will be my successor here in your house. When I am dead and gone, that lady will perhaps—

NORA. Hush! Not so loud; she is in there.

RANK. To-day, as well? There, just what I said!

NORA. Only to put my costume in order. Dear! dear! how absurd you are. (*Sits on the sofa.*) Now, do just be sensible, Doctor Rank; to-morrow you shall see how beautifully I dance, and then you may fancy, if you like, that I am doing it all to please you only,—and of course Torvald as well ;—of course. (*Takes various things out of the cardboard box.*) Doctor Rank, sit over here ; and then I will show you something.

RANK (*sitting down*). What is it ?

NORA. Look here. Do you see these ?

RANK. Silk stockings.

NORA. Flesh-coloured. Aren't they lovely ? Oh, it's so dark here now ; but to-morrow . . . No, no, no, you must only look at the feet. Oh, very well, you may look at the rest, too.

RANK. H—m.

NORA. What are you looking so critical about ? Don't you think they would fit me ?

RANK. It is impossible I should have any settled opinion on that point.

NORA (*looks at him a moment*). For shame. (*Hits him lightly on the ear with the stockings.*) Take that for it ! (*Rolls them up again.*)

RANK. And what other splendid things have you got there, that I was to see ?

NORA. You won't be allowed to see anything more, for you don't behave nicely. (*She hums a little, and searches among the things.*)

RANK (*after a short silence*). When I am sitting here in such perfect intimacy with you, I can't imagine—in fact, I can't form the slightest idea, what would have become of me, if I had never entered this house.

NORA (*smiling*). Yes, I really think you thoroughly like being with us.

RANK (*more softly, looking straight before him*). And now I must go away from it all.

NORA. Nonsense. You won't go away from us.

RANK (*in the same tone*). And not be able to leave behind me the smallest sign of thanks; scarcely a passing thought of regret,—nothing but an empty place, which can be filled by the next comer as well as by anybody else.

NORA. And if I were to ask you now for . . . No !

RANK. For what?

NORA. For a great proof of your friendship.

RANK. Well, well?

NORA. No, I mean,—for a very, very great service.

RANK. Would you really for once, make me so happy as all that?

NORA. Oh, you have no notion yet, what it is.

RANK. Very well ; then tell me directly.

NORA. But I can't, Doctor Rank : it is such an extraordinarily great thing; both advice, and help, and a service.

RANK. The greater the better. I can't imagine what you can mean. But do go on. Don't you trust me ?

NORA. Yes, as I trust nobody else. You are my best and most faithful friend. I know that. For that reason, I will tell you what it is. Well, then, Doctor Rank, there is something which you must help me to hinder. You know how deeply, how indescribably Torvald loves me ; he would not hesitate a moment to give his very life for mine.

F

RANK (*bending towards her*). Nora, do you think, then, that he is the only one who would—

NORA (*with a slight start*). Who?—

RANK. Who would gladly give his life for you?

NORA (*sadly*). Oh!

RANK. I had sworn that you should know it, before I went away for ever. I should never find a better opportunity. Yes, Nora, now you know it. And now you know, too, that you can trust yourself to me, as you could to no one else.

NORA (*stands up simply and calmly*). Let me pass, please.

RANK (*makes way for her, but sits still*). Nora.

NORA (*in the door to the hall*). Ellen, bring the lamp. (*Walks to the stove.*) Oh, dear Doctor Rank, that was really too bad of you.

RANK (*standing up*). That I have loved you devotedly, as no one else does? Was that too bad of me?

NORA. No; but that you should go and tell me so. It was really not necessary . . .

RANK. What do you mean? Did you know it, then?

(Ellen *comes in with the lamp, sets it down on the table, and goes out again.*)

RANK. Nora,—Mrs. Helmer,—I ask you, did you know anything of it?

NORA. Oh, what do I know, as to whether I knew or didn't know? I really can't say . . . But that you could possibly be so clumsy! Everything was going on so beautifully.

RANK. Well, at any rate you know now for certain, that I am quite at your disposal, soul and body. So will you speak plainly?

NORA (*looking at him*). Speak on, now?

RANK. I beg you to tell me what it is you want.

NORA. Now I can say nothing to you.

RANK. Oh yes, yes! you must not punish me in that way. Give me leave to do for you whatever is in human power.

NORA. You cannot do anything for me, now. Besides, I really want no help. You will find it was only my imagination. Yes, that is all. Of course. (*Sits in the rocking-chair, looks at him, smiles.*) Yes, you really are a charming gentleman, Doctor Rank. Now just tell me, aren't you ashamed of yourself, now that the lamp is on the table?

RANK. No, indeed I am not. But perhaps I ought to go, and for ever?

NORA. No; you certainly needn't do that. Of course you are to come to us as you always have come. You know very well that Torvald can't do without you.

RANK. Yes; but you?

NORA. Oh, I always think it is immensely delightful when you come.

RANK. That is just what led me to mistake my path. You are a riddle to me. It often seemed to me, as though you would almost as gladly spend your time with me as with Helmer.

NORA. Yes,—don't you see? there are some people whom one loves most; and other people whom one would almost always prefer spending one's time with.

RANK. Ah, there's some truth in that.

NORA. When I was still a girl at home, I naturally loved papa best. But I always thought it was immensely amusing when I could steal into the maids' room; for they never lectured me, and they always talked so entertainingly amongst themselves.

RANK. Oh, I see; then it is *their* place I have taken.

NORA (*jumps up and goes towards him*). Oh! dear, good Doctor Rank, I never meant that. But you can very well imagine, that I feel about Torvald just as I used to feel about father.

(Ellen *comes in from the hall.*)

ELLEN. If you please, ma'am. (*Whispers in her ear, and gives her a card.*)

NORA (*glances at the card*). Ah! (*Puts it in her pocket.*)

RANK. Something disagreeable up?

NORA. No, not in the least. It is only something; —it is my new costume.

RANK. How can it be? There's your dress.

NORA. Oh, that one, yes; but it's another, that . . . I ordered it . . . Torvald is not to know.

RANK. Oh, indeed. So that's the great secret!

NORA. Yes, to be sure. Do just go into his room; he is in the inner room; do keep him as long as you can.

RANK. Make yourself easy; he sha'n't get away from me. (*He goes into* Helmer's *room.*)

NORA (*to* Ellen). Then he is waiting in the kitchen?

ELLEN. Yes; he came to the back door.

NORA. But did you not tell him I had a visitor with me?

ELLEN. Yes, ma'am; but it was no use.

NORA. He really will not go away, then?

ELLEN. No, ma'am; not until he has spoken with you.

NORA. Then let him come in, but quietly. Ellen, you must not tell any one; it is a surprise for my husband.

ELLEN. Oh yes, ma'am; I quite understand. (*She goes out.*)

NORA. The terrible thing is coming. It is here already. No, no, no; it can never happen; it shall not. (*She goes to* Helmer's *door and slips the bolt.*)

(Ellen *opens the hall door to* Krogstad, *and shuts it behind him. He wears a travelling coat, high boots, and a fur cap.*)

NORA (*towards him*). Speak quietly. My husband is at home.

KROGSTAD. All right; I don't care.

NORA. What do you want of me?

KROGSTAD. An explanation of something.

NORA. Be quick, then. What is it?

KROGSTAD. You know I have received my dismissal.

NORA. I could not prevent it, Mr. Krogstad. I fought to the last on your behalf; but it was no use.

KROGSTAD. Does your husband love you so little? He knows what it is that I can expose you to, and yet he dares—

NORA. How can you suppose he has got to know it?

KROGSTAD. Oh! no; I didn't think that, either. To show so much manly courage did not look much like my fine Torvald Helmer.

NORA. Mr. Krogstad, I demand respect for my husband.

KROGSTAD. To be sure; all due respect. But since you, dear madam, are so anxious to keep the matter secret, I suppose I may venture to assume, that you are a little clearer than you were yesterday, as to what you have really done?

NORA. Clearer than *you* could ever make me.

KROGSTAD. Yes, such a bad lawyer as I am!

NORA. What is it you want?

KROGSTAD. Only to see how you were getting on, Mrs. Helmer. I have been thinking about you all day long. A cashier, a scribbling newspaper writer, a—in short, a creature like me, nevertheless, has a little bit of what people call 'heart,' you know.

NORA. Then show it; think of my little children.

KROGSTAD. Did you and your husband think of mine? But let's leave that alone. I only wanted to tell you, that you needn't take this matter too seriously. I sha'nt be the first one to talk about it.

NORA. No; to be sure. I knew you wouldn't be.

KROGSTAD. It can be settled as amicably as possible. Nobody need know. It can remain among us three.

NORA. My husband is never to know anything about it.

KROGSTAD. How can you prevent that? Can you pay off the debt, eh?

NORA. No, not at once.

KROGSTAD. Or have you any means of raising the money in the next few days?

NORA. No means that I will make use of.

KROGSTAD. And if you had, it would have been no good to you. If you stood here with ever so much money in your hand, you wouldn't get your I. O. U. back from me.

NORA. Then tell me what you want to do with it.

KROGSTAD. I only want to keep it, to have it in my own hands. No one whom it does not concern shall hear anything of it. If, on account of it, you were to form any desperate resolution . . .

NORA. As I do.

KROGSTAD. If you should think of leaving your husband and children . . .

NORA. As I do.

KROGSTAD. Or if you should think of doing something far worse . . .

NORA. How do you know that?

KROGSTAD. —then leave it alone.

NORA. How do you know I am thinking of doing that?

KROGSTAD. Most of us think of *that* as the first thing to do. I thought of it too; but really had not the courage.

NORA (*noiselessly*). Nor I.

KROGSTAD (*relieved*). No; one hasn't. You have not the courage either, have you?

NORA. I haven't; I haven't.

KROGSTAD. Besides, it would be very silly. When

the first storm is only over in the house . . . I have a letter for your husband, here in my pocket.

NORA. Telling him everything?

KROGSTAD. Sparing you as far as possible.

NORA (*quickly*). He shall never have that letter. Tear it up. I will get you the money somehow.

KROGSTAD. I beg your pardon, Mrs. Helmer; but I thought I had just told you . . .

NORA. Oh, I'm not talking about the money I owe you. Tell me how large a sum you demand from my husband, and I will get it for you.

KROGSTAD. I demand no money from your husband.

NORA. What *do* you want, then?

KROGSTAD. I will tell you. I want to get on in the world, dear madam; I want to redeem my position in it. And your husband shall help me to do it. For the last eighteen months, I have not been concerned in any dishonourable transaction; during that time, I have been fighting against the most straightened circumstances. I was content to work my way up, step by step. Now I am turned out; and I am not satisfied to get employment again, as a matter of favour. I mean to rise in the world, I tell you . . . I will get into the Bank again,—and in a higher position than before. Your husband shall make a place on purpose for me.

NORA. He will never do that.

KROGSTAD. He will do it. I know him; he won't dare to object. And when I am once associated with him there, you will soon see! Before a year is out, I shall be the manager's right hand. It will be Nils

Krogstad, and not Torvald Helmer, who carries on the Joint Stock Bank.

NORA. You shall never bring that to pass.

KROGSTAD. Perhaps you would . . .

NORA. Yes; now I have the courage for it.

KROGSTAD. Oh, you don't frighten me. An elegant, spoilt lady like you . . .

NORA. You will see; you will see.

KROGSTAD. Under the ice, perhaps. Down into the cold, coal-black water? And then next spring, be fished up on the shore, ugly, unrecognizable, with your hair all fallen out . . .

NORA. You don't frighten me.

KROGSTAD. Nor you me. People don't do things of that sort, Mrs. Helmer. And, after all, what would be the use of it? I should have your husband here in my pocket, just the same.

NORA. Even then, still? When I am no longer—

KROGSTAD. Do you forget, that even then, your forgery would still be in my hands? (*Nora stands speechless and looks at him.*) Well, now you are prepared. Do nothing foolish. So soon as Helmer has received my letter, I shall expect to hear from him. And bear in mind, that it is your husband himself who has forced me back again into such paths. That I will never forgive him. Good-bye, Mrs. Helmer. (*He goes out through the hall.*)

NORA (*goes to the door, opens it a little, and listens*). He is going. He is not putting the letter in the box. No, no, it would be quite impossible. (*Opens the door further and further.*) What does that mean?

He is standing still, not going down the stairs. Is he thinking better of it? Would he? (*A letter falls into the box;* Krogstad's *steps are then heard, until lost in the distance down the stairs.*)

NORA (*with a suppressed cry rushes through the room to the sofa-table; short pause*). In the letter-box! (*She steals across to the door.*) There it lies. Torvald, Torvald, now we are lost.

MRS. LINDEN (*comes with the costume from the left room*). Well, now, I can't see anything more to put right. Should we just try it on?

NORA (*hoarsely and softly*). Christina, do come here.

MRS. LINDEN (*throws the dress on the sofa*). What's the matter? You look so disturbed.

NORA. Do come here. Do you see that letter? There, see! through the wire-work of the letter-box.

MRS. LINDEN. Yes, yes; I see it.

NORA. That letter is from Krogstad.

MRS. LINDEN. Nora, it was Krogstad who lent you the money.

NORA. Yes; and now Torvald will know all about it.

MRS. LINDEN. Oh! believe me, Nora, it is the best thing for you both.

NORA. You don't know all yet. I have forged a name.

MRS. LINDEN. Good heavens!

NORA. I only wanted to tell you that, Christina; that you might be my witness.

MRS. LINDEN. How 'witness'? What am I to—?

NORA. If I go mad; and that might easily happen.

MRS. LINDEN. Nora!

NORA. Or if anything else should happen to me,—anything such as my not being able to be here present . . .

MRS. LINDEN. Nora, Nora, you seem quite out of your mind.

NORA. In case there were to be anybody who wanted to take the . . . the whole blame, you know . . .

MRS. LINDEN. Yes, yes; but how can you think . . .

NORA. Then you will be able to bear witness, that it is not true, Christina. I am not in the least out of my mind. I am in full possession of my senses; and I say to you: Nobody else knew anything about it; I alone have done everything. Don't forget that.

MRS. LINDEN. I won't forget it. But I haven't the remotest notion what it all means.

NORA. Oh, how should you? Why! what will come to pass now, will be a miracle.

MRS. LINDEN. A miracle?

NORA. Yes, a miracle; but it is so terrible, Christina. It must not happen for anything in the world.

MRS. LINDEN. I will go straight off to Krogstad, and talk to him.

NORA. Don't go to him. He will pain you in some way.

MRS. LINDEN. There was a time, when for love of me, he would have done anything.

NORA. He?

MRS. LINDEN. Where does he live?

NORA. Oh, how can I tell? Yes. (*Feels in her pocket.*) Here is his card. But the letter, the letter!

HELMER (*in his room knocks at the door*). Nora!

NORA (*cries out anxiously*). Yes; what is it? What do you want with me?

HELMER. Well, well, don't be so frightened. We aren't coming in; you have bolted the door, you know. You are trying your dress on, I dare say?

NORA. Yes, yes; I'm trying it on. It suits me so well, Torvald.

MRS. LINDEN (*who has read the card*). So he lives close by here, at the corner?

NORA. Yes; but it's no use now. We are lost. The letter is actually in the box.

MRS. LINDEN. And your husband has the key?

NORA. Yes, always.

MRS. LINDEN. Krogstad must ask to have his letter back unread. He must make some excuse—

NORA. But this is the very time when Torvald generally—

MRS. LINDEN. Prevent him; go and stay with him all the time. I will come back as quickly as I can. *She goes away quickly through the hall door.*)

NORA (*goes to* Helmer's *door, opens it, and peeps in*). Torvald.

HELMER (*in the back-room*). Well, now, may one come back into one's own room? Come, Rank, now we'll just have a look. (*In the door.*) But what does this mean?

NORA. What, Torvald dear?

HELMER. Rank led me to expect a grand dress-transformation scene.

RANK (*in the door*). So I understood; but I was mistaken, too.

NORA. No; before to-morrow evening, nobody will get any opportunity of admiring me in my splendour.

HELMER. But, dear Nora, you look so tired. Have you been practising too hard?

NORA. No, I haven't practised at all yet.

HELMER. But you really must.

NORA. Yes, it is quite indispensable, Torvald. But I can't get on at all, without your help; I have completely forgotten the whole thing.

HELMER. Oh, we'll soon freshen it all up again.

NORA. Yes, do help me at last, Torvald. Will you promise me that? Oh! I am so anxious about it! Before such a large party! You must sacrifice yourself entirely to me this evening. You mustn't do a scrap of business, or take a pen in your hand. Say 'yes.' Am I not right, Torvald dear?

HELMER. I promise you: all this evening, I will be at your entire disposal. You little helpless thing!—hm, it is true there is just one thing I will first— (*Goes towards the hall door.*)

NORA. What do you want outside there?

HELMER. Only to see if any letters have come.

NORA. No, no, don't do that, Torvald.

HELMER. But why not?

NORA. Torvald, I beg you not to; there are none there.

HELMER. Let me just see. (*Will go.*)

(Nora, *at the piano, plays the first bars of the Tarantella.*)

HELMER (*standing still in the door*). Ah!

NORA. I can't dance to-morrow, if I don't try it
over with you.

HELMER (*going to her*). Are you really so afraid,
dear Nora?

NORA. Yes, so dreadfully afraid. Let me try it at
once; we have a little time left before dinner. Oh!
sit down here and accompany me, Torvald dear; set
me right; guide me, just as you always do.

HELMER. With all the pleasure in life, since you
wish it. (*He sits down to the piano.*)

NORA (*takes the tambourine out of the box, and
also a long gay shawl, with which she drapes herself very rapidly; then with a bound, she comes to
the front of the stage*). Now, you play, and I will
dance.

(Helmer *plays*, Nora *dances; Rank stands at the
piano behind* Helmer *and looks on.*)

HELMER (*playing*). Slower, slower!

NORA. I can't do it differently.

HELMER. Not so violently, Nora.

NORA. That is just its style.

HELMER (*stops*). No, no; it isn't right.

NORA (*laughs and swings the tambourine*). Isn't that
just what I told you?

RANK. Let me play for her.

HELMER (*rising*). Yes; do so; then I can guide
her better.

(Rank *sits down to the piano and plays.* Nora *dances*

more and more wildly. Helmer *stands by the fire and addresses frequent remarks in correction, during the dance. She seems not to hear them. Her hair gets loose and falls on her shoulders; she does not heed it, but goes on dancing. Mrs.* Linden *enters.*)

MRS. LINDEN (*stands as though spell-bound in the doorway*). Oh !

NORA (*dancing*). It is merry enough here, Christina.

HELMER. But, dearest, sweetest Nora, you are dancing as if it were a matter of life and death.

NORA. And so it is.

HELMER. Rank, just stop; this is the merest madness . . . Stop, I say.

(Rank *stops playing, and* Nora *comes to a sudden standstill.*)

HELMER (*going towards her*). I should never have believed it. You have positively forgotten everything I taught you.

NORA (*throws the tambourine away*). You see it for yourself.

HELMER. You really do want teaching.

NORA. Yes ; now you see how needful it is. You must practise with me up to the last moment. Will you promise me that, Torvald ?

HELMER. You may certainly rely upon my doing so.

NORA. Neither to-day nor to-morrow must you think about anything but me ; you must not open a single letter,—not so much as the letter-box.

HELMER. Oh, you are still afraid of that man.

NORA. Yes, I am.

HELMER. Nora, I can see it in your manner. There is a letter from him in the box now.

NORA. I don't know ; I believe so. But you are not to read anything of that sort ; nothing of a worrying kind must come between us, until everything is over.

RANK (*softly to* Helmer). You mustn't contradict her.

HELMER (*putting his arm round her*). The child shall have her own way. But to-morrow night, when you have danced—

NORA. Then you will be free.

ELLEN (*in the right doorway*). Dinner is ready, ma'am.

NORA. We will have some champagne, Ellen.

ELLEN. Yes, ma'am. (*Goes.*)

HELMER. Dear, dear ; quite a banquet !

NORA. Yes, a champagne banquet until morning dawns. (*Calls out.*) And maccaroons, Ellen ;—plenty —a great many—just this once !

HELMER (*taking her hands*). Come, come, not this awful wildness ! Be my gentle little lark, once more.

NORA. Oh, yes, I will. But now go into the dining-room ; and you too, Doctor Rank. Christina, you must help me to do my hair.

RANK (*softly as they go*). There is nothing in the wind ? Nothing . . . I mean . . .

HELMER. Nothing whatever, my dear Rank. It is merely this babyish anxiety I was telling you about. (*Both go to the right.*)

NORA. Well ?

MRS. LINDEN. He is gone out of town.

NORA. I saw it in your face.

MRS. LINDEN. He only returns to-morrow evening. I left a note for him there.

NORA. You should have left it all alone. You ought not to hinder anything. After all, there is something glorious in expecting a miracle to happen.

MRS. LINDEN. What do you expect, then?

NORA. Oh, you can't understand. Go to them in the dining-room; I'll come in a moment. (Mrs. Linden *goes to the dining-room*.)

NORA (*stands a while, as though collecting her thoughts. Then looks at her watch*). Five;—seven hours before midnight. Then twenty-four hours before the next midnight. Then the Tarantella will be over. Twenty-four and seven. Still thirty-one hours to live.

HELMER (*in the right-hand door*). But what has become of the little lark?

NORA (*runs with open arms towards him*). Here is the lark.

ACT III.

(*The same room. The sofa-table, with the chairs round it, has been moved forward into the middle of the room. A lamp is burning on the table. The door to the hall stands open. Dance music is heard from overhead.*)

(Mrs. Linden *sits by the table and turns the pages of a book absently. She tries to read, but seems unable to fix her attention ; occasionally she listens, and looks anxiously towards the hall door.*)

MRS. LINDEN (*looking at her watch*). Not here yet ! And it is the latest time I mentioned. If he only doesn't . . . (*Listens again.*) Oh, there he is ! (*She goes into the hall and opens the corridor door carefully ; a light tread is heard on the steps. She whispers*) Come in. Nobody is here.

KROGSTAD (*in the doorway*). I found a note from you at my house. What does that mean ?

MRS. LINDEN. It is absolutely necessary I should speak with you.

KROGSTAD. Indeed ? And was it absolutely necessary the interview should take place here ?

MRS. LINDEN. It was impossible at my lodgings. I have no sitting-room to myself. Come in ; we are quite alone. The servant is asleep, and the Helmers are at the ball, overhead.

KROGSTAD (*peering into the room*). Ah! what? The Helmers are dancing this evening? Really?

MRS. LINDEN. Yes. Why not?

KROGSTAD. Quite right. Why not?

MRS. LINDEN. And now, Mr. Krogstad, let us talk a little.

KROGSTAD. Have we two anything left, to say to each other?

MRS. LINDEN. We have a great deal to say.

KROGSTAD. I should not have thought so.

MRS. LINDEN. Because you have never really understood me.

KROGSTAD. Was there anything more to understand, than what was the plainest fact in the world? A heartless woman jilts a man, when a better match offers itself.

MRS. LINDEN. Do you consider me so utterly heartless? Do you think I should have broken it off with a light heart?

KROGSTAD. Didn't you?

MRS. LINDEN. Did you really think that of me, Nils?

KROGSTAD. If it wasn't so, why did you write me such a letter as you wrote at the time?

MRS. LINDEN. I really could not do otherwise. Since I had to break with you, surely it was also my duty to destroy in your heart everything you felt for me.

KROGSTAD (*clasping his hands together*). So that

was it.   And all,—all for the sake of money,
only.

MRS. LINDEN. You ought not to forget, that I had
a helpless mother and two little brothers.   We could
not wait for you, Nils ; at that time, you had but poor
prospects.

KROGSTAD. Very likely ; but you had no right to
turn me off for the sake of any other man.

MRS. LINDEN. Oh, I don't know.   I have asked
myself often enough since, whether I had the right to
do it.

KROGSTAD (*more gently*). When I had lost you, it
seemed to me as though the very ground had sunk
away from under my feet.   Just look at me : I am a
shipwrecked man on a raft, now.

MRS. LINDEN. I should think some help was close
at hand.

KROGSTAD. It *was* at hand ; but then you came and
stood in my way.

MRS. LINDEN. Without knowing it, Nils.   It was
only this morning I learnt, that it was your post I had
got at the Bank.

KROGSTAD. I believe you, since you say so.   But
now you do know it, do you not mean to give
it up ?

MRS. LINDEN. No ; for that would not help you in
the least.

KROGSTAD. Oh, 'help,' 'help.'   I should do it,
whether or no.

MRS. LINDEN. I have learnt to act prudently.   Life,
and hard, bitter necessity have taught me to do so.

KROGSTAD. And life has taught me not to trust fine speeches.

MRS. LINDEN. Then life has taught you a very sensible thing. But I suppose you do trust deeds?

KROGSTAD. What do you mean by that?

MRS. LINDEN. You said you were like a shipwrecked man on a raft.

KROGSTAD. I had good reason to say so.

MRS. LINDEN. I am like a shipwrecked woman on a raft, too: no one to regret, and no one to care for.

KROGSTAD. You made your own choice.

MRS. LINDEN. I had no choice at the time.

KROGSTAD. Well, what more?

MRS. LINDEN. Nils, how would it be, if we two shipwrecked people could come over to each other?

KROGSTAD. What do you say?

MRS. LINDEN. Two people have better chance of being saved on a raft, than if each stays on his own.

KROGSTAD. Christina!

MRS. LINDEN. Why do you think I came here, to town?

KROGSTAD. Was it with some thought of me?

MRS. LINDEN. I must work, in order to endure life. All my days, so far back as I can remember, I have worked; and work has been my best and only joy. But now I am quite alone in the world,—so terribly empty and forsaken. There is no happiness in working for one's self. Nils, give me somebody and something to work for.

KROGSTAD. I don't trust that one bit. It is nothing but a woman's exaggerated notion of generosity, leading her to sacrifice herself.

MRS. LINDEN. Have you ever noticed any exaggeration in me?

KROGSTAD. What? You really could? Tell me, do you know all about my past?

MRS. LINDEN. Yes.

KROGSTAD. And do you know my reputation?

MRS. LINDEN. You hinted it just now, as though you meant, that with me you could have been another man.

KROGSTAD. I am perfectly certain of it.

MRS. LINDEN. Could it not yet be so?

' KROGSTAD. Christina, do you say this after full deliberation? Yes, you do. I see it in your face. Then you really have the courage?

MRS. LINDEN. I need somebody to mother, and your children need a mother. We two are necessary to each other. Nils, I believe in the nobler part of your nature. With you I dare attempt anything!

KROGSTAD (*seizing her hands*). Thank you, thank you, Christina. Now I shall know how to set about raising myself in the eyes of others. Oh, but I forgot . . .

MRS. LINDEN (*listens*). Hush! the Tarantella! Go, go.

KROGSTAD. Why, what is it?

MRS. LINDEN. Don't you hear the dancing overhead? When that is over, they will come back.

KROGSTAD. All right; I'll go. But it's too late

now. Of course you don't know what it is I have set going against the Helmers?

MRS. LINDEN. Yes, Nils, I know.

KROGSTAD. And nevertheless you have the courage to . . .

MRS. LINDEN. I can quite understand to what lengths despair may drive a man like you.

KROGSTAD. Oh, if I could but undo it again!

MRS. LINDEN. You could, for your letter lies there in the box.

KROGSTAD. Are you sure?

MRS. LINDEN. Yes; but . . .

KROGSTAD (*looking at her searchingly*). Is that the explanation of it? You want to save your friend at any price. Say it straight out. Is that the way the land lies?

MRS. LINDEN. Nils, a person who has once sold herself for the sake of others, never does it again.

KROGSTAD. I will ask to have my letter back again.

MRS. LINDEN. No, no.

KROGSTAD. Yes; I shall wait here till Helmer comes down. I shall tell him, that he is to give me my letter back; that it merely relates to my dismissal, and that he had better not read it.

MRS. LINDEN. No, Nils, you must not ask for the letter back.

KROGSTAD. But tell me, wasn't that the very reason for your fixing to meet me here?

MRS. LINDEN. Yes, in my first moment of terror. But since then, more than twenty-four hours have gone by; and during that time, I have heard things in this

house, which are beyond belief. Helmer must know
everything; this unhappy secret must come to light;
between those two, there must be the completest
possible understanding; and that can never come to
pass, while all these concealments and subterfuges are
going on.

KROGSTAD. Very well, since you are so bold. But
there is one thing I can do, at any rate, and it shall be
done at once.

MRS. LINDEN (*listens*). Make haste; go, go. The
dance is over; we are not safe another moment.

KROGSTAD. I will wait for you in the street, in front
here.

MRS. LINDEN. Yes, do. You must take me home.

KROGSTAD. Oh! I never was so wildly happy, in all
my life before. (*He goes out through the outer door.
The door between the room and the hall remains
open.*)

MRS. LINDEN (*sets the furniture a little straight, and
puts her walking things together*). What a change! what
a happy change. Somebody to work for, to live for!
a deserted home to bring comfort into! Well, he will
be an easy prisoner . . . . If only they would come
soon. (*Listens.*) Ah, here they are! Where are my
things? (*She puts on her bonnet and cloak.*)

(Helmer's *and* Nora's *voices are heard outside; a
key is turned in the lock, and* Helmer *leads* Nora *almost
forcibly into the hall. She wears the Italian costume,
with a large black shawl over it. He is in evening
dress, with an open black domino.*)

NORA (*still in the door, struggling with him*). No,

no, no; I won't go in; I want to go upstairs again.
I don't want to leave the ball so early . . .

HELMER. But, dearest Nora—

NORA. Oh, I do beg and pray you, so earnestly,
Torvald,—I beg you so very much; only one more
hour.

HELMER. Not another minute, my sweet Nora. You
know we settled it should be this way. Nora, go into
the room; you are catching cold here.

(*He leads her gently into the room, in spite of her
resistance.*)

MRS. LINDEN. Good evening.

NORA. Christina!

HELMER. What, Mrs. Linden, you here so late?

MRS. LINDEN. Yes, pardon me; I did so want to see
Nora in her costume.

NORA. Have you been sitting here, waiting for
me?

MRS. LINDEN. Yes. Unfortunately, I did not come
early enough. You were already gone upstairs; and
then I thought I could not go away again, without
seeing you.

HELMER (*taking Nora's shawl off*). Yes, look at her
well. I should rather think she was worth looking at.
Is she not beautiful, Mrs. Linden?

MRS. LINDEN. Yes, I must say—

HELMER. Is she not wonderfully lovely? That was
the general opinion at the ball. But she is dreadfully
obstinate,—dear little creature! What is to be done
with her? Will you believe it, I had almost to use
force to get her away from the ball?

NORA. Oh, Torvald, you will be sorry you did not grant my wish, even if it was only for half an hour longer.

HELMER. There! you hear her, Mrs. Linden? She dances her Tarantella, wins wild applause,—which, however, was but due to her, although perhaps her rendering was a little too realistic; I mean ... a little more than could be reconciled with the strict demands of art. But be that as it may, the chief thing was she got applauded, wildly applauded. Ought I to have let her stay after that, and weaken the impression? Not if I know it. I took my charming Capri maiden,—I might say my capricious little maiden from Capri,—under my arm; a rapid turn round the room; bows from all sides, and, as they say in novels—the lovely apparition was gone. A departure should always be effective, Mrs. Linden; but I can't get Nora to see it ... By Jove, it's warm here. (*Throws his domino on a chair and opens the door to his room.*) What? It's very dark here. Yes, of course; pardon me. (*He goes inside and lights two candles.*)

NORA (*whispers quickly and breathlessly*). Well?

MRS. LINDEN (*softly*). I have spoken to him.

NORA. And—?

MRS. LINDEN. Nora ... You must tell your husband everything.

NORA. I knew it.

MRS. LINDEN. You have nothing to fear from Krogstad; but you must speak.

NORA. I shall not speak.

MRS. LINDEN. Then the letter will.

NORA. Thank you, Christina. Now I know what I must do. Hush!

HELMER (*coming back*). Well, Mrs. Linden, have you admired her?

MRS. LINDEN. Yes; and now I will say good-night.

HELMER. What, already? Does this knitting belong to you?

MRS. LINDEN (*taking it*). Yes, thanks; I was nearly forgetting it.

HELMER. Then you do knit?

MRS. LINDEN. Yes.

HELMER. Do you know, you ought to embroider instead?

MRS. LINDEN. Indeed! Why?

HELMER. Because it looks far better. Look now. You hold the embroidery in the left hand, in this way, and then move the needle with the right hand,—in and out,—in an easy, long-shaped bow, don't you?

MRS. LINDEN. Yes, I dare say you do.

HELMER. While in knitting, on the contrary, it can never be anything but ugly. Look now; your arms are bent tightly together, and the needles go up and down; there is something Chinese in it . . . Oh! that really was splendid champagne they gave us!

MRS. LINDEN. Now, good-night, Nora, and don't be obstinate any more.

HELMER. Well said, Mrs. Linden.

MRS. LINDEN. Good-night, Mr. Helmer.

HELMER (*going with her to the door*). Good-night, good-night. I hope you'll get safely home. I would gladly . . . but it really is not far for you. Good-night, good-night. (*She goes. He shuts the door behind her and comes in again.*) There, now we've shut the door on her. She is an awful bore.

NORA. Aren't you very tired, Torvald?

HELMER. No, not in the least.

NORA. Nor sleepy?

HELMER. Not a bit. On the contrary, I feel most lively. But you? Yes, you look really tired and sleepy.

NORA. Yes, I am very tired. I shall soon be asleep now.

HELMER. There now, you see. I was right, after all, in not stopping longer with you at the ball.

NORA. Oh, all is right that you do.

HELMER (*kisses her on the forehead*). That is my dear little lark speaking like a human being. But did you notice how merry Rank was this evening?

NORA. Oh, was he really? I had no opportunity of speaking with him.

HELMER. Nor had I, much; but I have not seen him in such good spirits for a long time. (*Looks at her for a little while, then comes nearer to her.*) Hm . . . but it is quite too supremely delightful to be back in our own home, for me to be quite alone with you. Oh, you enchanting, glorious woman!

NORA. Don't look at me in that way, Torvald.

HELMER. I am not to look at my dearest treasure? —all the glory that is mine, mine only, wholly and altogether mine.

NORA (*goes to the other side of the table*). You must not talk to me in that way this evening.

HELMER (*following her*). I see, you have the Tarantella still in your blood; and that makes you more
enchanting than ever. Listen: the other guests are
beginning to go now. (*More softly.*) Nora, soon all
the house will be still.

NORA. Yes, I hope so.

HELMER. Yes; don't you, my own darling Nora?
Oh, do you know, when I go into society with you, in
this way, do you know why I speak so little to you,
and keep at such a distance from you, and only steal
a glance at you now and then,—do you know why I
do it? Because I am fancying, that you are one whom
I love in secret, that I am secretly betrothed to you,
and that nobody guesses there is any particular understanding between us.

NORA. Yes, yes, yes; I know very well, that all
your thoughts are with me.

HELMER. And then, when we have to go home, and
I put the shawl about your dear young shoulders, and
this glorious throat of yours, I imagine you are my bride,
and that we are coming straight from our wedding, and
that I am bringing you for the first time to my home,
and that I am alone with you for the first time, quite
alone with you, you shy, beautiful thing. All this
evening I was longing for you, and you only. When
I watched you chasing and beckoning during the
Tarantella, it seemed to set my blood on fire; I could
endure it no longer . . . and that's why I made you
come home with me so early.

NORA. Go now, Torvald; you must leave me alone.
I won't have all that.

HELMER. What can you mean? You must be joking with me, Nora dear. You 'won't'; 'won't'? Am I not your husband? (*There is a knock at the front door.*)

NORA (*recovering herself*). Do you hear?

HELMER (*going to the hall door*). Who is there?

DOCTOR RANK (*outside*). It is I. May I come in for a moment?

HELMER (*in a low tone, annoyed*). Oh, dear, what can he want at this time of night? (*Aloud.*) Wait a little. (*Goes and opens the door.*) Come, it is nice of you not to pass by our door.

RANK. I thought I heard your voice, and that made me long just to look in. (*Glances rapidly round the room.*) Yes, here is the dear place I know so well. It is so quiet and comfortable here, with you two.

HELMER. You seemed to enjoy yourself a good deal upstairs, too.

RANK. Exceedingly. Why should I not? Why shouldn't one take everything as it comes in this world? At any rate, as much and as long as one can. The wine was excellent.

HELMER. Especially the champagne.

RANK. Did you notice it, too? It was almost incredible the quantity I contrived to drink.

NORA. Torvald drank a great deal of champagne this evening, too.

RANK. Did he?

NORA. Yes; and after it, he is always in such a good temper.

RANK. Well, why should one not have a merry evening after a well-spent day?

HELMER. Well-spent? As to that I have not much to boast of, I am sorry to say.

RANK (*tapping him on the shoulder*). But I have, don't you see?

NORA. Then you have certainly been engaged in some scientific investigation, Doctor Rank.

RANK. Quite right.

HELMER. Just see! here's little Nora talking about scientific investigations.

NORA. And am I to congratulate you on the result?

RANK. By all means, you must.

NORA. Then the result was a good one.

RANK. The best possible, alike for the physician and the patient,—namely, certainty.

NORA (*quickly and searchingly*). Certainty?

RANK. Complete certainty. Ought not I, upon the strength of it, to be very merry this evening?

NORA. Yes, you were quite right to be, Doctor Rank.

HELMER. I say the same,—provided you don't have to pay for it to-morrow.

RANK. Well, in this life, nothing is to be had for nothing.

NORA. Doctor Rank, I am sure you are very fond of masquerade balls?

RANK. Yes, when there are plenty of interesting masks present.

NORA. Listen, and tell me what we two ought to appear as, at our next masquerade.

HELMER. You giddy little thing, are you thinking already about your next ball?

RANK. We two? I will tell you. You must go as the lucky fairy.

HELMER. Yes; but think of a costume to suit the character.

RANK. Let your wife appear in her every-day dress.

HELMER. That was really said very nicely. But don't you know what character you will take yourself?

RANK. I am perfectly clear as to that, my dear friend.

HELMER. Well?

RANK. At the next masquerade, I shall appear invisible. (*)

HELMER. What a comical idea !

RANK. Don't you know there is a big, black hat — haven't you heard stories of the hat, that made people invisible? You pull it all over you, and then nobody sees you.

HELMER (*with a suppressed smile*). Oh, I dare say.

RANK. But I am quite forgetting why I came in here. Helmer, just give me a cigar,—one of the dark Havannas.

HELMER. With the greatest pleasure. (*Hands him the case.*)

RANK (*takes one and cuts the end off*). Thanks.

NORA (*strikes a fusee for him*). Let me give you a light.

RANK. Thank you. (*She holds the match. He lights his cigar at it.*) And now, good-bye.

HELMER. Good-bye, good-bye, my dear fellow.

NORA. Sleep well, Doctor Rank.

RANK. I thank you for that kind wish.

NORA. Wish me the same.

RANK. You? Very well, since you ask me:—sleep well And thank you for the light. (*He nods to them both and goes.*)

HELMER (*in an undertone*). He'd been drinking a good deal.

NORA (*absently*). I dare say. (Helmer *takes his bunch of keys from his pocket and goes into the hall.*) Torvald, what are you doing out there?

HELMER. I must empty the letter-box;—it is quite full; or there will be no room for the newspapers to-morrow.

NORA. Are you going to do some work now?

HELMER. You know very well I shan't! What's this? Somebody's been at the lock.

NORA. The lock?

HELMER. Yes, most certainly somebody has. What does it mean? I could never believe, that the servants . . . Here's a broken hair-pin. Nora, it is one of yours.

NORA (*quickly*). Then it must have been the children.

HELMER. Then you really must break them of such tricks. Hm, hm. There! at last I've got it open. (*Takes the contents out and calls into the kitchen.*) Ellen, Ellen; just put the hall door lamp out.

(*He returns to the room and shuts the door into the hall. With letters in his hand.*) Just see! only look how they have accumulated. (*Looks among them.*) What's that?

NORA (*at the window*). The letter! oh, no, no, Torvald!

HELMER. Two visiting cards,—from Rank.

NORA. From Doctor Rank?

HELMER (*looking at them*). Rank, M.D. They were on the top. He must have put them in, when he went away.

NORA. Is there anything on them?

HELMER. Over the name, there is a black cross. Look at it. That is a very ominous sign. Upon my word, it is as though he were announcing his own death.

NORA. So he is.

HELMER. What! do you know anything? did he tell you anything?

NORA. Yes. He said, that when the card came, it would mean he had taken leave of us. He means to shut himself up and die.

HELMER. Poor fellow! I did know, that I should not be able to keep him much longer. But so soon! . . And then he goes into his hiding-place, like a wounded animal.

NORA. If it has to happen, it is best for it to happen without words; is it not, Torvald?

HELMER (*walking up and down*). He was so thoroughly intimate with us. I can hardly fancy our life without him. He and his troubles and loneliness formed a sort of cloudy background to our sunny happiness. Well, perhaps it is best so—for him, at any rate. (*Stands still.*) And perhaps for us, too. Now we two are thrown entirely upon each other. (*Puts his arm round her.*) My darling wife! it seems to me as if I could never hold you closely enough. Do you know, Nora, I often wish some danger might threaten you, against which I could stake body and soul, and all, all else, for your dear sake.

NORA (*frees herself and says firmly and decidedly*). Now you shall read your letters, Torvald.

HELMER. No, no, not to-night. I want to stay with you, sweet wife.

NORA. With the thought of your friend's death?

HELMER. You are right, dear. It has shaken us both. Something unlovely has come between us: thoughts of death and dissolution. We must try to get rid of them. Till then,—you go to bed, and I will go to my room a little.

NORA (*her arms round his neck*). Torvald, good-night, good-night.

HELMER (*kisses her on the forehead*). Good-night, my little singing bird. Sleep well, Nora. Now I will go and read all my letters through. (*He goes into his room with the bundle of letters, and shuts the door behind him.*)

NORA (*with wild glances, wanders round touching things, seizes* Helmer's *domino, throws it over her, and whispers quickly, hoarsely, and brokenly*). Never see him again! Never, never, never! (*Throws her shawl over her head.*) And never see the children again! Not them, either! Never, never. Oh, that black, icy water! Oh, that bottomless . . . Oh, if it were but over! Now he has it; now he is reading it.

Oh, no, no ; not yet. Torvald, good-bye, you and the children.

(*She is rushing out through the hall ; in the same moment* Helmer *tears his door open and stands there, with an open letter in his hand.*)

HELMER. Nora !

NORA (*crying aloud*). Ah !

HELMER. What is this ? Do you know what is in this letter ?

NORA. Yes, I know. Let me go ; let me go out.

HELMER (*holding her back*). Where do you want to go to ?

NORA (*tries to get free*). You shan't save me, Torvald.

HELMER (*falling back*). True ! is it true what he writes ? Horrible ! No, no ; it is perfectly impossible, that it can be true.

NORA. It is true. I have loved you beyond all else in the world.

HELMER. Don't come to me with silly excuses.

NORA (*a step nearer to him*). Torvald !

HELMER. You miserable creature !—what have you done ?

NORA. Let me go. You shall not bear it for my sake ; you shall not take it upon yourself.

HELMER. Don't try any actress's tricks. (*Shuts the door to the hall.*) Here you will stay and account to me for this. Do you comprehend what you have done ? Answer. Do you understand it ?

NORA (*looks at him fixedly, and says with hardening*

expression). Yes. Now I begin to understand it quite—

HELMER (walking round). Oh, what an awful awakening! During all these eight years,—she who was my joy and my pride—a hypocrite, a liar,—ay, and worse, worse—a criminal. Oh! what a depth of wickedness it implies! Ugh! ugh!

(Nora is silent, and continues to look fixedly at him.)

HELMER (continues standing before her). I ought to have guessed, that something of the kind was sure to happen. I ought to have foreseen it. Your father's careless principles,—be silent!—your father's careless principles you have inherited, every one of them. No religion, no morality, no sense of duty! Oh, how bitterly punished I am, for ever having winked at his doings. I did it for your sake, and this the way you reward me.

NORA. Yes, this is the way.

HELMER. You have utterly destroyed my happiness; you have ruined my whole future. Oh, the thought of it is fearful! I find I am in the power of a human being, who is devoid of conscience; he can do whatever he pleases with me, ask of me whatever he chooses, order me about, and command me exactly as it suits him;—I shall not dare to complain . . . And I must sink in this pitiable way and go to ruin, for the sake of an unprincipled woman.

NORA. When I am no more, you will be free.

HELMER. No dramatic effects, if you please. Your father was always ready with fine phrases of that kind. What good would it do me, if you were 'no more,' as

you say? No good in the world! In spite of that, he
can publish the whole story; and if he does publish
it, perhaps I should be suspected of having been a
party to your criminal transactions. Perhaps people
would think I was the originator, that I prompted you
to do it. And for all this I have you to thank,—you
whom during the whole of our married life, I have so
cherished. Do you understand now what it is you
have done for me?

NORA (*with cold calm*). Yes.

HELMER. It is so incredible, that I can hardly
believe it. But we must come to some decision.
Take that shawl off. Take it off, I say! I must try
to pacify him, in some way or other. The story must
be kept a secret, cost what it may. And so far as you
and I are concerned, it must appear, that we go on as
we always have gone on. But of course, only in the
eyes of the world. Of course, you will continue to
live in the house; that is understood. But the
children I shall not allow you to educate; I dare not
trust them to you . . . Oh, that I should have to say
this to one whom I have so tenderly loved . . . whom
I still . . . But that must be a thing of the past.
Henceforward, there can be no question of happiness,
but merely of saving the ruins, the fragments, the
appearance of it. (*There is a ring at the hall door.*
Helmer *recovers himself.*) What's that? So late!
Can it be the most terrible thing of all? Can he? . . .
hide yourself, Nora; say you are ill. (Nora *stands
motionless.* Helmer *goes to the hall door and opens
it.*)

ELIAS (*half-undressed in the hall*). Here is a letter for mistress.

HELMER. Give it to me. (*Seizes the letter and shuts the door.*) Yes, it is from him. You shall not have it. I will read it myself.

NORA. Read it.

HELMER (*by the lamp*). I have hardly courage to. Perhaps we are lost, both you and I. Well! I must know. (*Tears the letter hastily open; glances through a few lines; looks at an enclosure; a cry of joy.*) Nora! (*Nora looks interrogatively at him.*) Nora! Indeed I must read it again. Yes, yes; it is so. I am saved! Nora, I am saved! ⁷.

NORA. And I?

HELMER. You too, of course; we are both saved, you and I. Look here. He sends you back your acknowledgment of the debt; he writes, that he regrets and laments,—that a happy turn in his life . . . Oh, it can't matter to us what he writes. We are saved, Nora! Nobody has any hold over you. Oh, Nora, Nora! Ah, but first let us destroy all these horrible pieces of writing . . . I'll just see, though. (*Glances at the I. O. U.*) No, I won't look at it; the whole thing shall be no more to me than a bad dream. (*Tears the I. O. U. and both the letters in pieces, throws them into the fire, and watches them burn.*) There, it has no further existence. He wrote, that ever since Christmas Day, you had been . . . Oh, Nora, they must have been three awful days for you!

NORA. I have fought a hard fight in the last three days.

HELMER. You must have tortured yourself and not seen any means of escape but . . . But we won't think about those ugly things any more; we will only rejoice and repeat: It is all over, all over. Do you hear, Nora; somehow you don't seem able to grasp it yet! Yes, it's over. Then what can be the meaning of this set look on your face? Oh, poor dear Nora, I quite understand: you can't believe just yet, that I have forgiven you. But I really have forgiven you, Nora; I swear it to you; I have forgiven you everything. I know so well, that what you did, was all done out of love to me.

NORA. That is true.

HELMER. You loved me just as a wife should love her husband. It was only the means you could not judge rightly about. But do you think you are less dear to me for not knowing how to act alone? No, indeed; only lean on me; I will advise you; I will guide you. I should be no true man, if this woman's helplessness did not make you doubly attractive in my eyes. You must not dwell on the harsh words I spoke, in my first moment of terror, when I believed ruin was about to overwhelm me. I have forgiven you, Nora; I swear to you I have forgiven you.

NORA. I thank you for your forgiveness. (*Goes through the right door.*)

HELMER. No, stay. (*Looks in.*) What are you doing in the alcove?

NORA (*inside*). Talking off my masquerade dress.

HELMER (*in the open door*). Yes, do, dear; try to rest and restore your mind to its balance, my scared little song-bird. You may go to rest in comfort, I have broad wings to protect you. (*Walks about close by the door.*) Oh, how beautiful and cosy our home is, Nora. Here you are safe; here I can shelter you, like a hunted dove, whom I have saved from the claws of the hawk. I shall soon quiet your poor beating heart. Little by little, it will come about, Nora; you will find I am right. To-morrow all that will look quite different to you; everything will soon be going on just as it used to do; I shall not need to repeat over and over again, that I forgive you: you will really feel for yourself, that I have done so. How can you think it could ever strike me to drive you away, or even so much as reproach you? Oh, you don't know what a true man's heart is made of, Nora! A man feels there is something indescribably sweet and soothing in his having forgiven his wife, that he has honestly forgiven her, from the bottom of his heart. She becomes his property in a double sense, as it were. It is as though he had brought her into the world again. She has become, to a certain extent, at once his wife and his child. And that is what you shall really be to me henceforth, you ill-advised and helpless darling. Don't trouble about anything, Nora: only open your heart to me, and I will be both will and conscience to you. Why, what's this? Not gone to bed? Have you changed your dress?

NORA (*entering in her everyday dress*). Yes, Torvald; now I have changed my dress.

HELMER. But why, now, so late?

NORA. I shall not sleep to-night.

HELMER. But, Nora dear . . .

NORA (*looking at her watch*). It is not so very late. Sit down here, Torvald. We two have much to say to each other. (*She sits on one side of the table.*)

HELMER. Nora, what does that mean? Your cold, set face?

NORA. Sit down. It will take some time. I have a great deal to talk to you about.

HELMER (*sitting opposite to her at the table*). Nora, you make me anxious. And I don't understand you.

NORA. No; that is just it. You don't understand me. And I have never understood you either, till to-night. No; you mustn't interrupt me. You must only listen to what I say . . . This is the settlement of an account, Torvald.

HELMER. How do you mean?

NORA (*after a short silence*). Does not one thing strike you as we sit here?

HELMER. What should strike me?

NORA. We have now been married eight years. Does it not strike you, that to-night for the first time, we two,—you and I, husband and wife,—are speaking together seriously?

HELMER. Well; 'seriously,' what does that mean?

NORA. During eight whole years and more, since the day we first made each other's acquaintance, we have never exchanged one serious word about serious things.

HELMER. Then would you have had me persistently initiate you into anxieties you could not help me to bear?

NORA. I am not talking of anxieties. All I am saying is, that we have never sat down together seriously, that we might try to get to the bottom of anything.

HELMER. But, dearest Nora, would it have been any good to you, if we had?

NORA. That is the very point. You have never understood me . . . I have been greatly wronged, Torvald. First, by father, and then by you.

HELMER. What! by us two,—by us two, who have loved you more deeply than all others have?

NORA (*shakes her head*). You two have never loved me. You only thought it was pleasant to be in love with me.

HELMER. But, Nora, these are strange words!

NORA. Yes; it is just so, Torvald. While I was still at home with father, he used to tell me all his views; and so of course I held the same views; if I had different ones, I concealed it, because he would not have liked it. He used to call me his little doll, and he played with me, as I used to play with my dolls. Then I came to live in your house.

HELMER. What expressions you do use to describe our marriage!

NORA (*undisturbed*). I mean,—then I passed over from father's hands into yours. You settled everything according to your taste; and so I had the same taste as you, or else I let it seem so; I don't exactly know. I think it was both ways, first one and then the other. When I look back on it now, it seems to me as if I had been living here like a poor man, only from hand to mouth. I have lived by performing tricks for you,

Torvald. But you would have it so. You and father have sinned greatly against me. It is the fault of you two that nothing has been made of me.

HELMER. Nora, how senseless and ungrateful you are! Haven't you been happy here?

NORA. No; that I have never been; I thought I was, but I never was.

HELMER. Not . . . not happy?

NORA. No; only merry. And you were always so kind to me. But our house has been nothing but a playroom. Here I have been your doll-wife; just as at home, I used to be papa's doll-child. And my children were, in their turn, my dolls. I used to think it was delightful when you took me to play with, just as the children were, whenever I took them to play with. That has been our marriage, Torvald.

HELMER. There is some truth in what you say, exaggerated and overdrawn though it may be. But henceforth, it shall be different. The time for play is gone by; now comes the time for education.

NORA. Whose education?—mine or the children's?

HELMER. Yours, as well as the children's, dear Nora.

NORA. Oh, Torvald, you are not the man to educate me into being the right wife for you.

HELMER. And *you* say that?

NORA. And I,—how have I been prepared to educate the children?

HELMER. Nora!

NORA. Did you not say yourself an hour ago, that *that* was a task you dared not entrust to me?

HELMER. In a moment of excitement. How can you lay any stress upon that?

NORA. No; you were perfectly right. For that task I am not ready. There is another which must be performed first. I must first try to educate myself. In that, you are not the man to help me. That I must do all alone. And that is why I am going away from you now.

HELMER (*jumping up*). What was it you said?

NORA. I must be thrown entirely upon myself, if I am to come to any understanding as to what I am and what the things around me are. So I cannot stay with you any longer.

HELMER. Nora, Nora!

NORA. I shall now leave your house at once. Christina will, I am sure, take me in for to-night . . .

HELMER. You are insane. I shall not allow that. I forbid you to do it.

NORA. There is no use in your forbidding me things, from this time forth. Whatever belongs to me I shall take with me. I will have nothing from you, either now or later on.

HELMER. What utter madness this is!

NORA. To-morrow I shall go home,—I mean to my old home. There it will be easier for me to get something to do, of one sort or another.

HELMER. Oh, you blind, inexperienced creature!

NORA. I must try to gain experience, Torvald.

HELMER. To forsake your home, your husband, and your children! And only think what people will say about it!

NORA. I cannot take that into consideration. I only know, that to go is necessary for me.

HELMER. Oh, it drives one wild ! Is this the way you can evade your holiest duties ?

NORA. What do you consider my holiest duties ?

HELMER. Do I need to tell you that ? Are they not your duties to your husband and your children ?

NORA. I have other duties equally sacred.

HELMER. No, you have not. What duties do you mean ?

NORA. Duties towards myself.

HELMER. Before all else, you are a wife and mother.

NORA. I no longer think so. I think that before all else I am a human being, just as you are ; or at least, I have to try to become one. I know very well, that most people agree with you, Torvald, and that books say something of the sort. But I cannot be satisfied any longer with what most people say, and with what is in books. I must think over things for myself, and try to get clear about them.

HELMER. Is it possible you are not clear about your position in your own family ? Have you not in questions like these, a guide who cannot err ? Have you not religion ?

NORA. Oh, Torvald, I don't know properly what religion is.

HELMER. What are you saying ?

NORA. I really know nothing but what our clergyman told me when I was confirmed. He explained, that religion was this and that. When I have got quite away from here, and am all by myself, then I will

examine that too. I will see whether what our clergyman taught is true ; or, at any rate, whether it is true
for me.

HELMER. Who ever heard such things from a young
wife's lips ? But if religion cannot lead you to the
right, let me appeal to your conscience. For I suppose
you have some moral feeling ? Or, answer me, perhaps
you have none ?

NORA. Well, Torvald, I think I had better not answer
you. I really don't know. My ideas about those things
are all upset. I only know, that I have quite a different
opinion about them from yours. And now I have learnt,
that the laws are different from what I thought they
were ; but I can't convince myself, that they are right.
It appears, that a woman has no right to spare her father
trouble, when he is old and dying, or to save her
husband's life. I don't believe that.

HELMER. You talk like a child. You don't understand the society in which you live.

NORA. No, no more I do. But now I will set to
work and learn it. I must make up my mind whether
society is right or whether I am.

HELMER. Nora, you are ill ; you are feverish ; I
almost think you are out of your senses.

NORA. I never felt so clear and certain about things
as I feel to-night.

HELMER. And feeling clear and certain, you forsake
husband and children ?

NORA. Yes ; I do.

HELMER. Then there is only one possible explanation of it.

NORA. What is that?

HELMER. You no longer love me.

NORA. No; that is just the thing.

HELMER. Nora! . . . Can you bring yourself to say so?

NORA. Oh, I'm so sorry, Torvald; for you have always been so kind to me. But I can't help it. I do not love you any longer.

HELMER (*keeping his composure with difficulty*). Is this another of the convictions you are clear and certain about?

NORA. Yes, quite certain and clear. That is why I will not stay here any longer.

HELMER. And can you also explain to me how I have lost your love?

NORA. Yes; I can, easily. It was this evening, when the miracle did not happen; for it was then I saw you were not the man I had taken you for.

HELMER. Explain yourself more; I don't understand.

NORA. I have waited so patiently all these eight years; for, indeed, I saw well enough, that miracles do not happen every day. Then this crushing trouble broke over my head; and then I was so firmly convinced, that now the miracle must be at hand. When Krogstad's letter lay in the box outside, the thought never once occurred to me, that you could allow yourself to submit to the man's conditions. I was so firmly convinced, that you would say to him, " Pray make the affair known to all the world ; " and when that had been done . . .

HELMER. Well? And when I had given my own wife's name up to disgrace and shame?

NORA. When that had been done, then you would, as I firmly believed, stand before the world, take everything upon yourself, and say, "I am the guilty person."

HELMER. Nora!

NORA. You mean I should never have accepted such a sacrifice from you? No; certainly not. But what would my assertions have been worth, compared with yours? That was the miracle which I hoped and feared. And it was to hinder it, that I wanted to put an end to my life.

HELMER. I would gladly work for you, day and night, Nora; bear sorrow and trouble for your sake; but no man sacrifices his honour to a person he loves.

NORA. That is what hundreds of thousands of women have done.

HELMER. Oh, you both think and talk like a silly child.

NORA. Very likely. But you neither think nor speak like the man I could agree with. When your terror was over,—not for what threatened *me*, but for what involved *you*,—and when there was nothing more to fear, then it was in your eyes, as though nothing whatever had happened. I was just as much as ever your lark, your doll, whom you would take twice as much care of in future, because she was so weak and frail. (*Stands up.*) Torvald, in that moment it struck me, that I had been living here, all these years, with a strange man,

I

and had borne him three children. Oh, I cannot bear to think of it. I could tear myself to pieces!

HELMER (*sadly*). I see it, I see it : a chasm certainly has opened between us . . . Oh ! but, Nora, could it not be filled up ?

NORA. As I now am, I am no wife for you.

HELMER. I am strong enough to become another man.

NORA. Perhaps, when your doll is taken away from you.

HELMER. Part—part from you ! No, no, Nora ; I cannot grasp it.

NORA (*going into the right room*). The more reason for it to happen. (*She comes in with her walking things and a small travelling bag, which she puts on the chair by the table.*)

HELMER. Nora, Nora, not now. Wait till to-morrow.

NORA (*putting on her cloak*). I cannot spend the night in the house of a man who is a stranger to me.

HELMER. But can't we live here as brother and sister ?

NORA (*tying her bonnet tightly*). You know quite well that would not last long. (*Puts her shawl on.*) Good-bye, Torvald. I will not see the children before I go. I know they are in better hands than mine. As I now am, I can be nothing to them.

HELMER. But later, Nora—later on ?

NORA. How can I tell ? I have no idea what will become of me.

HELMER. But you are my wife,—both as you are now, and as you will become.

NORA. Listen, Torvald. When a wife leaves her husband's house, as I am doing, then I have heard he is free from all duties towards her in the eyes of the law. At any rate, I release you from all duties. You must feel yourself no more bound by anything than I feel. There must be perfect freedom on both sides. There! there is your ring back. Give me mine.

HELMER. That too?

NORA. That too.

HELMER. Here it is.

NORA. Very well. Yes; now it is all past and gone. I will put the keys here. The maids know how to manage everything in the house far better than I do. To-morrow, when I have started on my journey, Christina will come, in order to pack up the few things, which I brought from home as my own. I will have them sent after me.

HELMER. Past and gone! Nora, will you never think of me again?

NORA. Certainly. I shall think very often of you, and the children, and this house.

HELMER. May I write to you, Nora?

NORA. No, never. You must not.

HELMER. But I may send you what . . .

NORA. Nothing, nothing.

HELMER. Help you, when you are in need?

NORA. No, I say. I take nothing from strangers.

HELMER. Nora, can I never become to you anything but a stranger?

NORA (*taking her travelling bag sadly*). Oh! Torvald, the greatest miracle of all would have to happen, then.

HELMER. Tell me what the greatest miracle is.

NORA. We should both need to change so,—you as well as I,—that—Oh, Torvald, I no longer believe in anything miraculous.

HELMER. But I will believe in it. Tell me. We must so change, that . . . ?

NORA. That our living together could be a marriage. Good-bye. (*She goes out through the hall.*)

HELMER (*sinks in a chair by the door, and puts his hands before his face*). Nora, Nora! (*He looks round and stands up.*) Empty. She isn't here now. (*A hope inspires him.*) The greatest miracle! (*Below-stairs is heard the dull sound of a door shutting in the lock.*)

THE END.

Richard Clay & Sons, Limited, London & Bungay.

CPSIA information can be obtained
at www.ICGtesting.com
Printed in the USA
LVHW110550131022
730617LV00006B/393

9 783337 188849